TAKE MY DRUM TO ENGLAND

by

DESMOND CORY

HODDER AND STOUGHTON
LONDON SYDNEY AUCKLAND TORONTO

Copyright © 1971 by Desmond Cory. First printed 1971. ISBN
0 340 15041 6. All rights reserved. No part of this publication may be
reproduced or transmitted in any form or by any means, electronic or
mechanical including photocopy, recording, or any information storage
and retrieval system, without permission in writing from the publisher.
Printed in Great Britain for Hodder and Stoughton Limited, St. Paul's
House, Warwick Lane, London, E.C.4 by Northumberland Press
Limited, Gateshead.

Highgate Cemetery. A fine rain falling.

"They put it up, you know."

"Who did, sir?"

"The Russians. Well, paid for it, anyway."

"I didn't know that."

"Ah, not everyone does. Not everyone does."

He turned away, hooking his neatly-furled umbrella over the crook of his arm, and they walked slowly, again in silence, down the gravel pathway. His black shoes gleamed in the brittle spring sunlight. The rain went on falling, softly.

"It's odd," Martin said eventually, "to see the old chap in a British cemetery. Isn't it? I mean—caused you a bit of trouble, one way or another."

Allanbee respectful, thoughtful. "I suppose he has."

"You've never read any of his stuff?"

"No. I'm not what you'd call a great reading man."

"Nor am I. And there again—though it sounds a bit strange, coming from me—I'm not really all that interested in politics. Never caught on to it, somehow. To each according to his need, how does it go? ... or was that Lenin? Human values, that's what count. Human values."

He stopped, peering intently down at the grave immediately to his left; a grave one would have thought—and Allanbee found—of no particular interest. Marble chips were sprinkled loosely between heavy grey fenders; a Corinthian-style headstone with a laurel-leaf motif. Karl Marx continued to stare at them from behind, gloomy in the sunlight and the rain. Visitors, always visitors. It wasn't so long since they'd blown him up. Nothing so exciting about these two.

Martin, with his umbrella and bowler hat. Why carry an umbrella, if you weren't going to use it when it rained? Lean, cadaverous, in his late fifties, his face seamed by a disfiguring scar. The other also thin and tall in a flapping grey raincoat, but very much younger, with an earnest, careworn expression; a student, a shop assistant ... He could have been anything. Nondescript. Nothing there to interest Karl Marx, who'd been dead, anyway, for nearly eighty years. "... Do you think much about death, Henry?"

"Not very much. Hardly at all."

"You're young, of course," Martin said. "But it doesn't do to forget it. Not altogether."

"I suppose ..." Henry stopped to think about it. He wasn't any too sure *what* he supposed, or what, irrespective of what he thought, would be the proper comment to make. "I suppose I think of it as something that comes to us all. Sooner or later. And there's nothing much that we can do about it."

"Absulit carum cita," Martin said, *"mors Achillem, longa Tithonum munit senectus ..."* He breathed out heavily through his long thin nose. "The young and the old. Comes to us all, oh, quite, quite. Quite."

"People nowadays seem to have so much else to think about."

The exhalation changed to a snort. "Yes, that's what they'll tell you. No time. Don't have time for anything. Rushing here, rushing there. Don't have time to remember the dead, let alone honour 'em. Don't have much time for the living, either, if you ask me. Too busy getting to the moon, burning down villages in Vietnam, too damned busy anyway. I don't believe a word of it myself. *You* find the time, don't you, Henry?"

"Well ...," Henry said mildly embarrassed.

"And I appreciate that. Believe me, I do. *Sacrifice*. That's

6

what people have forgotten. The spirit of sacrifice. Giving up something to help other people. Time, especially. Now *that*'s what it's really all about."

Martin expressed himself very obliquely at times, Henry thought. Right now, God alone knew what he was on about. He sounded, on these occasions, very like a schoolmaster. Henry found it very difficult to converse with him, but then, Henry found it difficult to converse with anybody. Now Martin had broken off, fortunately, in order to blow his nose on a large white handkerchief; a two-shilling piece, falling from its folds at the precise moment of detonation, impinged happily on the marble fender and rolled a yard or two down the path. The effect was that of a conjuring trick at an old-fashioned children's party. Henry retrieved the coin and returned it to its owner. "Comes to us all," Martin said, replacing both coin and handkerchief in his overcoat pocket. "Just so."

He paused, one hand raised slightly as though about to make materialise a hard-boiled egg; walked on a few yards and stopped again. Henry had by now lived long enough in Spain to recognise this stop-go process as a characteristic old Spanish custom. Martin hadn't been to Spain since 1937, had indeed spent in England half the time that Karl Marx had spent in the tomb, and was indeed in speech and to all outward impression a typical middle-aged middle-class Englishman of comfortable means ... Nevertheless there were habits of his youth—such as this one, precisely—that still persisted.

His innate tendency to freedom of gesture had been forgotten or, more probably, deliberately been suppressed, nor was his face particularly expressive; but, talking as now with some casual acquaintance, he stood perhaps a little closer than would, with an Englishman, be natural, and his eyes at times would crinkle, as at the recollection of a clear blue sky and a blazing sun. He could have passed, even so, for some minor creation of Maugham or even of

7

Buchan, back in the Old Country after a spell in South Africa or the F.M.S.; the scar curling down his cheek might have strengthened that impression. And rarely, very rarely indeed, did this impersonation carry an undertone of caricature. An interesting chap, when all was said and done. A pity that when he talked he was such a bore.

"This fellow we lost last year," Martin said. "A very brainy chappie indeed. Classical scholar at Oxford. My word, yes. The trouble with him was lack of discipline. A brilliant mind, but fundamentally undisciplined. And so of course he came to a sticky end."

"They caught him?"

"They didn't catch him, no. They never found his body; or if they did, it hasn't been reported. He probably got away and died of his wounds, poor sod. It's a good place for dying, Spain. Bags of space to do it in."

"Am I his replacement?"

"In a way."

The headstones all around them, the grey stone crosses. The sunlight had faded now, but the rain still fell; drops of it clung to Henry's thick fair hair. "How are you getting on with Cipriano?"

"We've only met a couple of times so far."

"That's right. You can't be too careful." Martin hesitated for a moment, perhaps on the verge of producing some other outworn Latin tag; in the event he refrained, or more probably it escaped him. "And Torrevedra? You're on top of the job there, I hope?"

"Nothing I haven't been able to handle. It's all fairly easy."

"Good. That's important too, you know. One could even say that's your first duty—to fit into the background. And it's a fairly pleasant job, or so I should imagine." He moved forwards again, the umbrella bumping awkwardly against his thigh. "Yes," Henry agreed. "It is."

8

"You're due back tomorrow?"

"That's right, sir."

"Yes. Well, memorise your instructions before you leave. Learn them thoroughly. And then burn them."

"I will."

Fancy being able to say something like that, absolutely straight-faced. And yet it sounded consistent, somehow; all a part of the stiff-upper-lip tradition. As though his cover story had permeated through into what, after all, he had to think of as being his real task in life. But then, why not? After all those years? It had to be difficult for him to distinguish between the real and the artificial Martin; perhaps indeed he didn't try to do so, not any more. Anyway Henry didn't know much about Martin. In fact he knew nothing of him, other than his name. It was better that way. Yes, they said that, too; portentously; but it was true. People did get caught. Memorise the instructions; burn them. Melodramatic, maybe; but all the same, that was exactly what Henry was going to do.

"You won't find it too difficult," Martin said. "Nobody's forgotten that you're still very much of a beginner."

They had reached the cemetery gate. Swains' Lane was ahead of them. Martin turned and held out his hand.

"That doesn't mean that we're not very glad to have you out there. You're going to be useful to us, Henry. Very useful."

The handshake, firm but slightly clammy; that of a man with a blood pressure problem, perhaps even a heart condition. Behind him stood the long rows of graves, fallen marble angels in every stage of collapse; an air of picturesque, almost of studied neglect. Highgate Cemetery. England. The British Empire. Decline and fall.

Martin walked away with long, eager strides now, his umbrella in his hand and briskly swinging. Henry, staring after him through the rain-mist, shook his head. Decline

9

and fall, indeed. Where better would you feel that than in a cemetery?

But in fact the whole of London had, to him, a funerary air. It didn't seem real. Over the past six months he had grown accustomed to Mediterranean clarity, to blue and brown and glittering grey and the hallucinatory blossoming of red; now London seemed in contrast a half-drowned Lyonesse, its colours muted by cold and swirling rain-currents, spider-webs of mist. Henry didn't like London, had never liked it. Somehow, it encouraged his dreams.

The 214 bus, swimming through the silvery shoals of evening traffic, buffeting against the blurred raindrops, eased up against the dark jetty of the pavement and stopped; "Tom Crow," the conductor said. Henry, hands in his raincoat pockets, disembarked. He bought a newspaper at a corner kiosk. POP STAR IN THIRD DAY OF COMA, the headline said. Girls without any clothes on stared at him from slightly above his eye-level, not in any great expectancy; they were last month's numbers and appeared to know it. Henry slipped the newspaper under his arm and walked away from the kiosk to the glass-and-metal cafeteria; it was early to eat and he wasn't very hungry, but later on the place would be crowded out. So would all the others. He took a corner table and ordered bacon and eggs and a cheese sandwich and then shook open the newspaper. *Third day of coma*, he thought. Yes, that about summed it up.

Martin might be worried about death; it was life that was chiefly Henry's problem. He was twenty-three years old and as yet he hadn't got it properly weighed off. This he found disturbing.

Loneliness. Death is infinite loneliness; hadn't somebody said that? Then death was the continuation of life by other means. A tide of humanity, pouring now over the bridges; walkers, stern-faced and fish-eyed, others in cars and buses; brief-cases, bowler hats, umbrellas; the lonely phalanxes. Going home, they'd have said. Better to go home early; find your place in the earth and stay there, six feet under. That was the sensible thing to do. The place would be crowded, later on.

Henry was twenty-three, but he hadn't yet given up. He hadn't yet become one of the walkers. That, at least, was how he looked at it. He hadn't given up yet. Not quite.

It didn't mean there was anything wrong with him. He was an ordinary chap, really. He was lonely because he chose to be. Human values, human relationships ... *that* was no kind of a problem. He could pick up a girl any place. Or a bird, rather. You called them "birds", now. There was one sitting at the counter, on a high revolving stool. Quite nice-looking. Mini-skirt, but they all wore mini-skirts nowadays. Henry went over and introduced himself and when she had finished her coffee they went out and round the corner to where Henry had his car parked—it was an E-type Jaguar, he rather thought—and they drove off at a tremendous lick, brakes screaming and all the rest of it, and her long blonde hair looked very nice, blown back by the slipstream. His bacon and eggs arrived and Henry began to eat them moodily. He *would* learn to drive one day, he decided. He would find it useful. Very useful.

He should have been thinking about what Martin had said, instead of about gir ... birds. He knew that very well. She wasn't his type, anyway. Not that he really knew what his type was; he'd never got around to speaking to any of them, except like that. Day-dreaming. A bad habit. Oh, he knew how to do it all right; everyone said it was easy. But he never got around to it. London, bloody London. He didn't like London. He hated it.

* * *

He turned sharp left into Leicester Square. The lights, the restaurants, the cinemas. In front of him a lean man, twenty feet tall, in a dark grey suit, clutched a pistol threateningly. The pistol was a Luger 9-millimetre Parabellum, very accurately drawn. In the background, girls again, and again virtually without any clothes on. In front of the tall man and staring at the pistol, a little man; five foot eleven, raincoated, carrying a folded newspaper. All you can see is his back, but not to worry. It's only Henry.

Outside the sentry-box, the soldier; red tunic and black bearskin; standing to attention. His eyes, like those of the girls on the paper-stand, focused on nothing. Henry didn't really envy him, but a soldier at least *belong*s to something. Companionship implies a shared belief.

It was getting dark. Henry came out of St. James' Street into the long bright scribble of the Piccadilly lights and waited at the crossing for the signal to flicker red. He saw the woman's face and her mouth coming open, but was still surprised when she started to scream; then brakes whimpered on wet asphalt and he heard a soft thump, as when a table is struck by an empty glove, though louder and heavier. The car stopped, rocking on its springs, one wheel up on the pavement, and there was a sudden crowd of people milling round the bonnet. The following traffic, a long line of it, was pulled up behind the twisted car and the lights were now on red, anyway. Henry walked across the road to the tube station and, more slowly, down the station steps. An accident. It's murderous, the traffic in London. Perhaps it was as well that he didn't have a car. And couldn't drive. Learning to drive, you sold out a little bit. The drivers were as bad as the walkers.

On the train, he tried to imagine that he'd imagined it. The accident. The woman's face. The scream. But it didn't work and he knew that it wouldn't work. Accidents had no part in the day-dream. He hated accidents and he hated thinking about them; but he couldn't help it. The scream was there in the rhythm of the train wheels; an accident, an *ac*-cident, an *ac*-cident. He tried to read his newspaper, but the vibration of the train made it difficult and his hands were trembling.

Looking out, all he could see was his own reflection in the darkened window.

1

Pleasant, Martin had said. Yes, the job was pleasant. And as he himself had said, not very difficult. Public Relations, was the answer he gave when people asked him; but people didn't ask very often. An acceptable phrase with no very obvious meaning.

There was an office, and outside the office were clumps of bright flowers; bougainvillaea clung to the whitewashed walls. There was a very high and very expensive hotel just behind; and behind the high hotel, the hills of the Sierra de Malaga. Scattered throughout those hills were the houses, the new houses; villas, chalets and bungalows with their connecting network of narrow roads. Torrevedra. The Village, it was called by those who lived there. Villages don't grow nowadays, don't accrete naturally; not on the Costa del Sol. They're planned and built by property speculators. That's why each one needs its office. The Torrevedra office was where Henry worked, where he had to "fit into the background". Martin, maybe, knew why. Henry didn't.

In fact he had the right qualifications. They'd wanted an Englishman at Torrevedra, because so many of the villagers were English, and even those who weren't—the Germans, the Dutch, the Swedes—spoke English, sometimes among themselves. Henry was the right kind of Englishman; he didn't have long hair and he'd been to a public school. His Spanish was very good indeed—his mother had been Spanish—and he was reasonably fluent in French. He spent much of his time making telephone calls in one or other of those three languages. He looked into complaints (there were usually plenty). He helped with the preparation of advertising brochures. And he sorted the mail. He was left with a good deal of free time.

"Plenty of people'd give their ears for a job like that."

"Yes," Henry said.

"Mind you, I can see there's no kind of a future in it. But then who cares about that? That's *mañana*, isn't it? Right on the sea, I suppose, this place of yours?"

"Torrevedra. Yes. About two hundred yards."

"Well, there you are then. All that swimming and boating and girls in bikinis. Let *mañana* look after itself. Oh yes—you're lucky."

Pleasant and not very difficult. You could call yourself a P.R.O. or you could call yourself the tea-boy; either fitted. And it didn't matter. The man in the seat beside him was small and intense and knew Spain extremely well; he spent a fortnight there every year. Last year, Benidorm. This year, Marbella. He'd be flying back to England in two weeks' time with a healthy tan, doubtless talking to someone else about the wonderful carefree Spanish philosophy of life. "These houses of yours—how much do they cost?"

"They usually sell the plot, initially. Then they'll build the house to your own design. Anything from fifteen to thirty thousand."

"Pricey," the man said. "Pretty pricey."

"Yes."

"And how do English people manage it?"

"There are different regulations," Henry said. "Dollar premiums and so on. But I don't know much about the legal side of it. We have a man who handles all that."

We have a man. It sounded all right, put that way. And after all, it was true. Santiago worked in the office like everyone else. For the organisation.

"And who's the boss? I mean, who runs the show?"

"A man called Martorell."

"Oh, yes. I've heard of him. Politician, wasn't he?"

"So I believe."

Of course it *was* an organisation. Property cartels are too big these days to be one-man firms; Torrevedra, S.A., had to have a good few millions wrapped up in it. Martorell was the boss, all the same; everyone knew it. And being the boss's son just had to help. You had to admit that Santiago knew his stuff; company law, conveyancing, all those complicated phrases beginning *o sea* ... He had it all at his fingertips. But all that red flannel about his being an employee like anyone else ... He wasn't. His name was Martorell. That was the point.

The other man leaned abruptly forwards to peer out of the window, thus breaking Henry's train of thought. The Trident was banking sharply, circling, a world of lion-coloured hills spinning reluctantly on its port wingtip. "Coming in to land," the other man said. "Ah, well. *Arriba España.*"

The people you meet on aeroplanes are always bores.

He sat on the edge of his bed for some little while, smoking one cigarette after another and making up a story about an aeroplane crash in which the sole survivors were himself and Elizabeth Taylor. Flying was another thing that Henry didn't much care for, and the trip from London had induced in him a nervous reaction—chiefly one of physical weakness. He was glad, all the same, to be back home.

Home was a small furnished flatlet in a block some five minutes' walk from the Torrevedra offices, a block where several other of the office employees lived. Though not, of course, Santiago. The flatlet had a bed-sitting-room and a kitchenette. Beside the bed was a small night table; on the night table, a telephone, an alarm clock and a glass of water, its contents flat and thickly filmed with dust. Henry had left for swinging London in rather a rush and had inadvertently left it standing there; he was usually careful about things like that. When he had crushed out the end of his third cigarette, he took the glass through to the kitchenette and emptied it and rinsed and dried it; then refilled it and carried it back to the night table. Then he sat down on the bed again, leaning back this time so that his head rested against the wall behind.

Apart from the bed and the table, there wasn't much furniture; but then there wasn't much space to put it in. There was a whitewood chest-of-drawers, unpainted, in the corner, and a room divider used as shelving because there wasn't any room to divide. There was a very new armchair with bright green plastic upholstery, already slightly ripped; and opposite the bed there was a built-in wardrobe with a full-length sliding mirror.

The flatlets in this block had been designed for people on holiday and foreigners at that; people who would naturally spend most of their days on the beach and most of their nights at Torremolinos. The rooms were comfortable enough, but claustrophobic. The office staff used them in the off-season, moving—in July and August—to the old, the *real* village some three miles away, but very few of them used the rooms for any other purpose than sleeping, at night and during the siesta hours. Henry, in this respect, was different. Henry was English. This room was his home and his home was his castle and in it, he'd sweat if he had to. It was the price one paid for privacy. Santiago, of course, had been the first to notice the fact and to make of it a subject for ribald comment. This, Henry tried to ignore. He hadn't much choice.

What made it home for Henry were Henry's things. His possessions. A few books on the bottom shelf of the room divider, mostly paperbacks; popular science, popular military histories, a few of the green Espasa-Calpe classics. And on the three upper shelves, his collection. Meticulously constructed scale models of military aeroplanes, rockets, tanks; all detailed and exact reproductions of their originals. It was a good collection. Henry had always been clever with his hands, even at school.

Ponsonby, he thought; (his eyes were now closed). Ponsonby had been the bastard's name. Even at school, some things had been the same; wherever you go, you run into the boss's son or his equivalent. The specially favoured. Santiago, to give him his due, was nothing like as bad as Ponsonby, as Ponsonby the blood, bloody Ponsonby. Sticking bits of wood together with glue; silly kid's game, that is. Supposed to be a tank, you say? ... Load of rubbish. I mean, tanks are strong. This isn't strong. (The strips of balsa cracking in his knobbly cricketer's hands, the carefully-razored panels tearing, splintering.) Not strong enough, is it, Dopey?

They call it dope, the glue you use. It had been a mistake all the same, telling them that. Dopey Allanbee, the model-aircraft crank. The Headmaster wants to see you, Dopey. You're in for it now, Dopey. You're in *real* trouble.

Trouble? ... No.

No trouble at all.

He's dead, is the only thing. He's dead at last. Ah, yes, Allanbee. Take a seat, will you ... Henry? Afraid I've some bad news for you. Some rather bad news. About your father. Sincerely sorry, Henry. We're sincerely sorry. You'll have to remember it's something that comes to us all.

Yes, sir. I understand, sir. Thank you, sir.

Then the Matron's room. Tea and biscuits in solace. But I didn't cry. Did I? I don't think so.

The last time I saw him was at Paddington Station. The school train, ready to pull out. I was standing at the window and so was able, for once, to look down on him. And on her. It was always *him* and *her*, never *them*. He was a big man and my mother, too, was tall; very tall, for a Spanish woman. They were having one of their usual fights and I wasn't even listening. It didn't seem important, I was worried about going back to school. I hated school. That wasn't surprising.

19

All the same, though, words got through. Some of them Hers, mostly; she had the shriller voice. *You can't keep her waiting much longer, can you? I don't know why you bother to hang around till the boy's train leaves* ...

In my hand were the two half-crowns, still warm from his pocket. I wished that the train *would* leave. In a way, it had; I'd been forgotten already. But my ghost still stood there looking down on her, on her sharp, contorted face, *One of these days I'll kill you ... and that bitch. I'll stick a knife in you both, believe you me* ...

Of course she didn't really mean it. She just talked that way. All the time. You certainly couldn't have called her a good-tempered woman. The steam was drifting in, down the platform. I couldn't see him now. Perhaps he'd gone. There were other voices, boys' voices, farther down the train, in another compartment. I held the half-crowns so tight that they started to hurt me.

Henry opened his eyes. He wasn't sure if he'd been asleep or not. He was sweating. He unbuttoned his shirt.

After a while he went over to the sideboard and pulled open the top drawer. Under his clean shirts, there was a pistol. It wasn't a model pistol. It was real. He pressed the magazine catch, checked that the magazine was loaded. Then he replaced it and pumped the bolt.

He sat down on the bed again with the pistol held loosely in his right hand. His head rested against the wall again, and again his eyes were closed. His wrist—arching, circling—brought the barrel of the pistol over and round until the tip of the muzzle touched his mouth; he parted his lips and bit at it gently, feeling the sick taste of the metal at the base of his tongue, numbing his throat. He pressed the trigger. It wasn't loaded. There was no risk. Just a dry, satisfying click. His head made of the wall behind him a sounding-board; the walls were thin, anyway, of hollow brick and plaster, and you could hear easily enough the footfalls of people passing down the corridor outside and sometimes, indeed, conversations in the neighbouring rooms. The footsteps that he heard now, following on the click, were quick and light and came to a halt outside his door. Henry opened his eyes in time to see the doorhandle begin a cautious ninety-degree turn and slipped the pistol underneath his pillow. He made no other move. The door opened.

Anita.

Well, *here's* a change of key.

Here she comes. Down the street. Long thin neck and tiny feet. A pretty little baby giraffe, a walking pop lyric and its name is Anita de la Vega y Alfonso. Great big eyes, but you can't see them because of the giant sun-glasses, and because of them she couldn't see Henry, either. Couldn't or, anyway, didn't. Her bare and brown and endless legs ambled her over to the wardrobe, which she opened. She rummaged about inside. She found almost at once what it was that apparently she wanted; a white-crowned Nazi officer's dress cap. This one stuck on her head at a rakish angle, then closed the wardrobe door to study the effect in the long mirror. In the mirror and behind her, Henry. Her face went suddenly long with fear, then crumpled up with relief. *"Ay—que susto me has dado."*

One hand pressed extravagantly to the underside of her left breast, easing, no doubt, the strain on her fluttering heart. An emotional little creature, Anita.

"You could always try knocking," Henry said.

"But I'd no idea you were back."

"I'm back."

"Well, nobody told me."

"What," Henry said, "do you think you're doing here, anyway?"

She touched the cap so that the peak tilted forwards over her nose. It suited her rather well, oddly enough. "I

21

thought you wouldn't much mind if I borrowed this. There's a party, you see—"

"You can't just walk into people's rooms and borrow things."

"Oh, come on, Henry, *no seas bobo*. Don't be so stuffy" She twitched her tight little behind over to the window, stared out of it, then waved frenziedly to someone invisible. "We're friends, aren't we?"

"Yes, but—"

"Friends and colleagues. All one big happy family. And how did you find them all, by the way, in England?"

"Fine," Henry said. No, it was impossible. Like trying to get sense out of a canary.

"Have a good time, did you?" Chipper, chipper.

"All right."

"What did you do?"

"I walked around a bit. Went to Highgate Cemetery."

"What's that?"

"It's a cemetery," Henry explained.

"Oh boy. So you went to a cemetery. You've really been swinging." She turned away from the window. "Me, I can wait till they carry me."

"It's quite an interesting place. Karl Marx is buried there."

"I can see that makes it the greatest. You'll have to tell me all about it sometime. But right now I have to run, people are waiting." Her face alive, alight with expectancy. A great time just around the corner. "Thanks for the cap, Henry. You're a sweetie."

"But—"

"I'll bring it back tomorrow. Promise."

She might. Then again, she might not. The door rattled shut behind her; her footsteps, running now, moved down the corridor. Bitch, Henry thought. She wouldn't always be able to get away with it. Ten years' time and she'd be a right old cow. Bloody cheek, was what it was. Coming in

22

here like that. Helping herself.

And then pulling all that friends and colleagues stuff. Colleague my eye. All she did was smile at people in the reception room and hand them right on to somebody else. Just office decoration. Leg art. With a good old family tree to back it up. Of course *that* didn't matter. The point was that there were plenty of other girls around who could do the job as well, or better, and who really needed the money. Anita didn't. Not with her allowance from her daddy the General. She certainly had enough money to buy her own fancy caps instead of stealing other people's. Stealing was what it came down to. And anyway she was a bitch. A stupid bitch.

He got up from the bed and went over to the window. The Thunderbird was drawn up almost directly beneath, and Anita was just getting into it. Henry knew very little about cars, but he did know a Thunderbird when he saw one; besides, he had seen that one before and knew who it belonged to. She was still wearing the cap. He could see the flat white circle of the brim against the scarlet upholstery.

The motor snarled up at him aggressively and off they roared, straight away from the pavement without bothering to signal. That, no doubt, would have been too bourgeois or something. Like knocking on doors. He watched the Thunderbird reach the end of the side road and start to swing left, on to the main artery. Then the T.N.T. charge wired to the differential went up and there was nothing there but a cloud of yellow-white smoke and a buckled balloon of blue metal. The sound of the bang reached him a full second later. Lucky, really, that the street had been empty.

Walking back to his bed, he changed his mind. Not T.N.T. A high-velocity rifle, that would be better. Her dark-haired head would explode to the impact of the bullet, would blow out a halo of blood; just for a second, there'd be a spray of corpuscular matter, of plasma so thin, so fine you could hardly see it. But the cap would be drenched with it. Henry had read about that happening. It was horrible, really.

Besides, he didn't really hate her. She was a stupid bitch, yes, but what he hated was just the *idea*, the idea of the world being full of women who'd love to be just like that, who'd like to be *her*. Things wouldn't usually need to be so very different. Then for them, too, it'd all be happening; the T-Bird with Santi Martorell at the wheel, the miniskirt lifting to show the right little flash of lace-edged pantie and of suntanned thigh, then the sun and the sea and the wind and the howl of acceleration and the wide grey road to Torremolinos. That's where the action is, baby. *Plenty of people'd give their ears for a job like that*. All men on 'planes are bores. All girls are stupid bitches.

He was lying now on the bed, eyes closed; his head on the pillow, the pistol beneath it. The half-crowns were clenched in his hand, so tightly that they'd begun to hurt him.

A twist of the wheel. That's all it takes. And the car's off the road, careering wildly, the windscreen shattered and the girl's scream soundless in the whip of the wind. That's what they don't show, the television commercials. That's what the papers don't say. He hadn't seen the cuttings, of course, till a long time after ... five years, was it? ... when his mother, too, had died. But then he'd found them pasted in a scrapbook, part of what the lawyer had called her "effects". She'd been a collector, too, of a kind.

STRIPPER KILLED IN CAR CRASH ...

Julie Wynter, her name had been. Quite a well-known name, apparently; some of the headlines had been in quite large print. But none of the cuttings had been very long. Most of them only mentioned the driver's name right at the bottom: James Allanbee. Also killed. Head-on into a lorry. Killed in the accident.

So she'd cut them all out with scissors and had pasted

them into a book. She'd been a collector, all right. And, even for a Spanish woman, a damned good hater. Now Henry could hardly remember her at all.

He had a little trouble the following morning with Mr. Petrie, who owned and—on occasion—occupied one of the more ostentatious villas, fronting on the sea. Mr. Petrie was a youngish longish-haired Londoner who had married, the previous year, a Swedish film star and who now derived what appeared to be a substantial income by taking pictures of his wife in the nude and selling them to various literary magazines. It wasn't this, of course, that was causing the trouble. The trouble had to do with his flowerbeds. Since the subsoil of his garden consisted principally of sand, a staggering show of blooms was hardly to be expected; Petrie's view, however, was that the gardener hadn't been trying. The gardener's name was Antonio. His view of the matter was simple, though rather monotonously expressed. "That's all very well," Henry said. "*You* say fuggem and *I* say fuggem, but someone's got to dig that bloody garden." "Not fuggin me," Antonio said. This admirable summary of Voltairean philosophy occupied, incredibly enough, almost the whole of Henry's morning. Or perhaps not incredibly at all. That was what the job was all about. That was what he was paid for.

There were, of course, possible sidelines. There had been, the week before his departure for London, the Italian lady. "What Italian lady?" Henry had asked.

"The one in the hotel. Second floor." Those were the more expensive suites. "The one with ... Plumpish, you might call her."

Yes, Henry remembered her vaguely. Name of Mazzantini or something. Rather a nice woman, he'd thought, but with tinted hair. Fiftyish. The motherly type. "What about her?"

25

"She's looking for someone, that's what about her."

"Looking for someone?"

"So I hear. English, preferably."

"Yes, but someone to do what?"

"Pero tu que crees?" Gomez had said. "Someone to stuff her crumpet, of course."

"But she's ... I don't believe it. You must be mistaken."

"Mistaken *ni ocho cuartos.* Well, why not? A thousand pesetas in it, at least, and probably a nice little present in the morning. Besides, she mightn't be bad. Not bad at all."

"Look, I'm sorry," Henry had said, preferring to ignore Gomez's culminating gesture. "It's not my line of country."

"Pues peor pa ti."

The stupid bastard. There were times when Henry thought that he'd make an excellent hater, too.

But there it was. The Torremolinos game. The beaches, the narrow plate-glass streets, Barbarella and Piper's Bang-Bang. Behind it all, the hotels with the luxury suites and the shaded rooms, the villas with asphalt drives and the lawns with whickering sprinklers, the tall drinks, the noisy all-night parties. But further still behind it all and looking down upon it, the bare ash-coloured hills powdery with dust, cracked by the hammering sun, the hills where nothing moved but the vectoring eagles. Henry felt, on mornings like this, a longing for the mountains, for the silence of the boulder-strewn arroyos, and walking down to Los Boliches along the four-lane highway he stopped and looked up and saw them there in the distance, the hills and the grey mountain summit, behind the beetle-glint and screech of the passing cars. In the Santa Cruz bar at the village centre he sat in the shade at the end of a seated row of tourists, blond beards and long beach-browned legs all crossed at the knees, and he thought, *It can't be invincible. Something must stop it. Then again there'll only be the mountains, the bleached bones of the hills and the marching sun.*

He remembered the detonators, lying on the work-bench. Slim metal cylinders. You could hit them with a hammer and they would explode with a sharp, ear-splitting crack and a strange acridity would hover for a few seconds in the air. Harmless, of course. He didn't really know whether the mountain was an earlier or a later memory; if he recalled the detonators as childhood toys, the mountain had that mysterious quality of having been always before him yet never there, something summoned from a pre-conscious state. But it had happened. Of course it had happened. The mountain was no dream.

He didn't know where and he didn't remember when. But it had been there, the mountain, on a dry day of fitful wintry sunlight; the jeeps drawn up at the base of it; the big men in khaki standing around in little groups, talking. He himself had been small and unobtrusive and had wished to be so, knowing that he had no business to be there, really, with these men, the Royal Engineers; so he had stood and had looked at the mountain for minutes on end, beginning, as often, to be bored, though overawed by his surroundings and by the company he was keeping. And then it had happened.

First the wisp of smoke, like an Indian signal, rising swiftly from the mountain peak. Then a narrow, boiling column leaping skywards, and at the foot of that column the slow, remorseless flowering of a bright red blossom. The tortured air was hammered outwards, vibrated overhead, collapsing to yield a huge crumpled ball of water vapour, a cloud from nowhere, half a mile across, while the whole mountain quivered in the haze of the screaming blast. The great red rose turned yellow and died while the smoke and steam poured upwards endlessly, as it seemed; and then, seconds afterwards, the voice of it reached him, the thundering tremble of high explosive, tons and tons of it, echoing from the war-cloud. Later came the breeze of it, damp and gentle against his face. That was what had awed

27

and staggered him—the slowness of it all. You expected sharpness, violence, the stinging crack of the detonator magnified; never this long, majestic, glorious unfolding, this revelation of a god-like power. On the way home he had asked—

"Did *you* do that, Dad?"

—unable to believe it. And now he had forgotten the answer, whatever the answer had been.

The truth was that even then he had known that his father, in initiating that tremendous experience, had not really "done it" at all, but had pressed down the charger as a priest might have held aloft the host—in the knowledge yet also, strangely, in ignorance of all that the act implied. In some ways this had been a difficult, an extremely abstract concept for a very young boy to have grasped—the idea of grace appertaining to office, held by virtue of a cloth crown sewn on a shoulder-strap. Yet somehow at that age he had seen what many grown-ups fail to comprehend—the irrelevance of that gift of grace to its recipient's individual worth. And he had understood, from then on, that a whisky priest is still and always a priest, that the pilots who had slaughtered women and children at Coventry and Dresden remained, while they held their commissions, officers and gentlemen, and that his father was invested—for all the fog of words about knives and bitches that blurred his outline—until the day of his violent death with a peculiar, an incomprehensible power. And insofar as the boy that had been Henry had felt an ambition, it had always been related to that search for office, for that gift of grace. Even to have been made a prefect would have been something. And yet that gift, for some reason, had been withheld until the money had run short and it had been too late. So here now he sat, just plain Henry Allanbee; not priest nor officer nor doctor nor advocate; snubbed by pretty receptionists, snapped at by junior managers, barely able, indeed, to hold his own in an argument with an under-gardener. Here he sat, quietly; yet burning. Burning with a slow, internal flame. He was the Revolution.

Cipriano came to sit beside him.

"*Buenas tardes*," Cipriano said.

Cipriano was the Revolution, too. But if he and Henry were ever to get to be friends, it wouldn't be on a basis of what they had in common. Cipriano was an electrical engineer. He installed most of the systems at Torrevedra and he earned good money. For the rest, he was twenty years older than Henry and had lived all his life in Spain; indeed, apart from two visits to Madrid he had never travelled farther north than Granada. He had no wish to go. He was nevertheless a widely-read and well-educated man. He had no wife and family. But he wasn't lonely.

He hadn't yet made his mind up what to make of Henry.

"I heard you were back."

"Yes," Henry said. "I got back yesterday."

"And how are things in London?"

"Much as usual."

Cipriano wondered, for a moment, what that meant. Cold, no doubt. And clinging fogs. Ugh. "And Martin?"

"He's very well. He sends you his regards."

"And ...?"

Memorise and burn. Henry's eyes, behind the tinted lenses of his sun-glasses, were still focused on the distant mountain peak. "You're to tell Ramona that the information from Sevilla is accurate. Ramona's now in Malaga. Calle del Principe, 42. It will be very soon now and Ramona will know when and will initiate action. That's the message."

"Any others?"

"No," Henry said.

It didn't seem very much to have gone all the way to London for. But Cipriano seemed satisfied.

'So," he said, "it looks as if the season's beginning. Again."

"What season?"

"The crusading season, *hijo*. We buckle on our sword belts and we sail for the Tierra Sagrada. Kill a Saracen or two. 'Initiate action'—yes, we know what *that* means."

"Is that how it's done?"

"Wave assault, they call it. It sounds very nice, in theory. A wave falls, and then there's a pause. A year, maybe two. Then another one comes. And in the end, down comes the cliff. It's the only way in which the weak can bring down the strong. It sounds good ... in theory."

"It takes a long time to bring down a cliff that way."

"You put your finger on the spot," Cipriano said. "With unerring acumen. It does. It takes a very long time indeed."

Over thirty years, so far. From one point of view, that wasn't so long; but from the vantage point of one man's lifetime, yes. A very long time. And the waves, visibly, were growing weaker. This year, it looked like being the Children's Crusade. The old ones, the good ones, the experienced ones were dead. So maybe it had to be that way. This year, Allanbee; foreigners they were sending now, English boys with baby faces. Perhaps that was to be expected.

Calle del Principe, 42 ...

"But then," he said, "Martin is a patient man."

"And you?"

"When I have to be."

A tall blonde in a white bikini came down the pavement, her sandals flopping on the hot asphalt. There were tiny drops of salt water still clinging to her walnut-brown body. Cipriano watched her pass in open and unrestrained admiration. Behind her, along the Malaga road, the sun glittered on the black shells of rows of cars, driving east, west, in two constant, hurried streams. "And of course," he said, "it isn't only us."

"You mean there are other organisations? Groups?"

30

"There are others, of course. Yes, quite a number. But I didn't mean them. It's just that I sometimes think," Cipriano said, "that the real revolutionaries are the capitalists. The ones who make our motor-cars, for example. *They*'re the ones who're turning Spain upside down. The big landed estates down here in the south ... They've been here for centuries. The politicians couldn't break them up. Not the Republicans. Not the Communists. But the motor-car will cut them to ribbons in another twenty years—just as in France and in Germany. It's just an idea I have. I'm a thinking man."

"As well as a patient man?"

"The two things go together."

"I don't know," Henry said. "There ought to be quicker ways."

The blonde, crossing the road. A blaze of hooters. On the mountain top, the red flower blossomed again in anger and in majesty; the cliff split, splintered, crumbled, fell away. Henry's eyes behind the tinted lenses blinked at the glare, while Cipriano watched the blonde break into a run. Worth waiting for that. Cipriano had, in fact, had quite a few successes among *las turistas*; he was big and he didn't *look* patient, and large impatient Spaniards have their appeal. He reached out his hand.

"I'll see you, Henry."

"*Hasta entonces*," Henry said.

Cipriano stood up and walked away, remembering:
Calle del Principe, 42.

Tell Ramona.

He knew Ramona.

Ramona was the case officer for the Pedro Hernandez job. That was *his* job. And Henry's, though Henry didn't know it.

Ramona was a good-looking woman, but one of the old ones; with each wave that fell, the old ones were fewer. Last year it had been Juanito Molina and Don Nico. They

31

said that Molina had committed suicide, but one could never be sure. And if this year's wave was planned to carry off Pedro Hernandez, it would be falling high up the beach; very high; higher than even Don Nico had ever gone. So next year, probably, the old ones would be fewer still. Not that it helped to think about it that way. It didn't help to think about it at all. But he, Cipriano, was a thinking man.

The blonde, again. Turning up the hill towards the villas, the white scrap of wet towelling bright in the sunlight, like a target flag. Cipriano stopped and turned his head, squinting at the hills, the distant mountain. Twelve miles or so to the north was a village where the *forasteros* didn't go, a hill village of tumble-down shacks and tall stone houses with a church and a half-dozen outlying smallholdings; there, not two months ago, an unmarried mother had been stoned to death. Upholders of the old tradition? Or bestial barbarians? Cipriano, lighting a cigarette, shook his head. Somewhere there had to be a balance; a balance between that bleeding, black-clad corpse and that other proud brown body in the white bikini. Somewhere, but not in Spain. In Spain, there were no half-measures.

He threw away the spent match, crossed the road and started up the path to the hotel. The blonde was moving more slowly now. The slope was steep. And Cipriano, fundamentally, was an optimist.

Four o'clock. The heat just past its maximum. And the errand-boy back on the job. Already those four days in London had disappeared into the past, had been swallowed in a gulp by the heat and dust and brilliance of the Costa del Sol. Back at the office, Gonzales, the junior architect, had a translation problem; Henry, at the typewriter, worked it out for him. The *supermercado* had a manifest to be checked. There were telephone calls from Malaga, Fuengirola, from Torre del Mar downcoast and one long-distance from Madrid. Two of the typists had a blazing row and Anita, at the reception desk, seemed to have a headache. Santiago didn't come in, and the people who had appointments to see him had to be told (by Henry, of course) to come back later. *Mañana*, maybe. They didn't like that very much. An ordinary sort of an evening, in fact.

Santiago rang through, in the end, a little before seven o'clock and said to bring round the papers that needed his signature. His rooms were on the top floor of the Torrevedra hotel, directly behind the office buildings; he had what amounted to a penthouse flat there. Santiago's P.A. was a fellow with a large moustache called Gomez (the man, not the moustache. This was Santiago's favourite joke and recurred about once every ten days; Gomez thought this joke extremely funny. Gomez was no fool). It was Gomez' job to take up the papers, but Gomez was on the point of going home to his own little flat in Fuengirola; Henry was also on the point of going off duty, but the hotel was conveniently on his way—Gomez said. Therefore, Henry could take the papers. As usual.

He got to the hotel at seven o'clock. The receptionist said that Don Santiago had gone out a moment before and had said that Mr. Allanbee was to wait. So Henry waited. He sat in the hotel lounge and read a newspaper which dealt at an inordinate length with the exploits of a local football team. He wasn't interested in football, but the chair was comfortable. At twenty to eight Santiago came in and thanked Henry effusively, his usual flashing smile much in evidence, and took the papers and put them away in his shiny brown leather brief-case. He'd sign them right away and then send them down and Henry could take them back to the office again. He wouldn't be long. *Tres minutos, nada más.* Henry sat down in the armchair again.

People were coming back from the beach, calling to each other in high, bird-like voices and mostly rather bad-temperedly, since they'd taken too much sun. Others, rather more completely attired, were leaving to dine and dance in Malaga and Marbella and Torre (you called it Torre, not Torremolinos, to show you were with it). For them there'd be restaurants, discotheques, night clubs, all conceivable kinds of high jinks. Henry put his newspaper aside and watched them flow in and out, wishing he could have a bath. The clock above the reception desk said eight-fifteen, and his wrist-watch said the same thing. It'd be no good asking the reception clerk to call Santiago with a polite reminder, because the clerk wouldn't do it. Henry knew this, because he'd tried before. So, of course, had Gomez.

But Cipriano wasn't the only one with patience. Spain is where you learn patience, as nowhere else; and, when all was said and done, the armchair was comfortable and the hotel lounge pleasant and cool. There were worse places to be. Henry had nowhere else to go, other than to his own small room. It was just that he would have liked to have a bath.

He felt sticky.

He went to stand for a while at the entrance to the foyer, watching the cars arriving and departing. The beach contingents were now all returned, because it was almost dark; there was no moon as yet, but a few stars had come out to the east. It was funny, what Cipriano had said about cars. Nowadays the car-owner was like Mark Twain's newsboy—greater than kings. The motor-car was progress. It couldn't be stopped. He watched the blue Alfa-Romeo nose in under the pergola and dim its powerful head-lights; Michael Petrie got out and, after a pause, Hanna, the car door slamming noisily behind her. Hanna was wearing, of course, her evening face, a flawless mask of make-up meticulously applied, flesh yet not flesh; under her sable wrap, black satin exposed most of her splendid breasts with an equal impersonal formality, as though they were on display in a shop window. Henry was scared stiff of Hanna Petrie. She spoke English well enough, with a breathless film-studio husk, but she didn't speak to him very often and she didn't speak to him now. Michael, following her to the lift, nodded briefly. Black tie, white dinner jacket; *he*'d found time to take a bath all right. Henry, sticky Henry, took off the sun-glasses that he'd forgotten he still had on and polished them industriously with a strip of Calotherm, then put them away in their zip-up case and stared at the reception desk clock. Half past eight. A pleasant job.

Some people would give their ears for it.

"*Ciao*, Henry."

He turned, mildly surprised. Another group of people were coming up the steps; among them, Anita. "Oh. Hullo." He nodded a deep Teutonic nod, bending fractionally at the waist; he often did this when slightly flustered.

'What are you doing here?"

Even if he'd been plying a shovel in the furnaces of hell and she'd appeared on the scene with a long forked tail, she'd say the same goddamned thing, *Hullo, Henry. What are you doing here?* Eyes wide open in moronic surprise . . . "Waiting," he said. "I have to pick up some papers."

"From Santiago?"

"Yes." That had to be obvious.

"But it's half past eight, *caramba*."

"Good Lord. So it is."

"Oh Henry. You're the limit. He won't be reading papers now, that's for sure. He's got a party on tonight." Glancing over her shoulder. The people with her had moved on, were waiting to enter the lift. "We're all going. I've got to run."

"Yes," Henry said. "Enjoy yourself."

She was turning away as he spoke. But then, for some

35

reason, she turned back. He saw that she'd had her hair done in some new way, all piled up on top of her head. Would that be what they called a chignon? ... "You're not going to go *on* waiting here, are you?"

"For a while, yes. I mean, they're important papers. Gomez said so."

"But it's long after hours. You're off duty."

"I've nothing else to do."

"He'll have forgotten about it." Biting her lower lip, a normal outward indication of profundity of thought. "Why don't you go on up and remind him about it? You know Santi. He'll only say, leave it till the morning. He's always doing that kind of thing."

"But I couldn't—"

"*Ay Dios, vamonos.*" She took him by the wrist and tugged him forwards. "I'll take you up there." "No, look," Henry said. "Really, I—"

"If you don't come, I'll scream."

She probably meant it. Half past eight and already she'd quite obviously been drinking. Henry felt considerably embarrassed. For her, of course, rather than for himself. Yes, she might easily scream. Nothing more likely. He shuffled along beside her over the carpet, his sleeve firmly crumpled in her small hot fingers. "Anita, you know I'd really much rather..."

"Waiting till half past eight. How wet can you *be*?"

She released his sleeve as soon as the lift doors had closed behind them. Whizzing upwards with a soft hydraulic swish, Henry said,

"I don't see how I can go in there. Above all if he's having a party, I'm not even dressed. I can't go *in*."

"I tell you what," Anita said. "We'll knock." And started to giggle like a schoolgirl. Henry had to resist a sudden and uncharacteristic impulse to bang her very hard over the head. "Why don't you just give him a message? Just say I'm waiting. Then all he has to do is 'phone downstairs—"

36

"Give's a kiss," Anita said.

"*What?*"

"You heard. A *big* kiss." And started giggling again, this time with her eyes closed. "Alone in a lift, Henry. Now's your chance."

"You're drunk," Henry said.

"I know. It's nice. It's smashing."

The lift stopped and her eyes came open again.

"Come on, then," she said. She sounded a bit abrupt, Henry thought.

"I'm sorry. I didn't mean it."

"Didn't mean what?"

"To say that. You're not drunk. Not really."

The door slid open, soundlessly. Anita took her finger off the button. "Ah, get stuffed," she said.

"What are *you* doing here?"

The question seemed a little more pertinent, coming from Santiago. "Yes," Henry said. "It's about—"

"You haven't got a drink. That's bad. That's very bad. That's dreadful. Help yourself, Henry. Bar's over there. Help yourself. God, you look beautiful tonight."

—this last sentence being addressed not, in fact, to Henry but to Hanna Petrie, into whose face Santiago was currently gazing from a range of about six inches, his arm being enfolded around her waist. The mask was as impassive as before, but her lower lip was now tucked under the white and regular row of her upper teeth, the more prominent of which were clearly visible. This probably meant that she was smiling; certainly not at Henry and not even demonstrably at Santiago, but smiling, anyway. Just smiling. "Gimme one too baby," Hanna said. Her English was always devoid of punctuation, as of any inflection, so was sometimes hard to understand. Not that it mattered.

"Eh?" Henry said. A *terrifying* woman.

37

"A drink, you fool, she wants a little drinkie." The small hot hand at his sleeve again, edging him towards the bar in the corner of the room. "And so do I. I told you everything would be all right."

The amplifier was above the bar and the noise was deafening. "That's not the point," Henry said. "I shouldn't—"

"What?"

"I shouldn't have—"

"He's nice, when you get to know him. Santiago. He just doesn't think. That's all."

"But I shouldn't—"

"After all, if *you* had that much money, maybe you wouldn't worry about other people either."

Henry was beginning to wonder if he would ever be allowed to complete a sentence again. He gazed at the wondrous array of bottles on the sideboard. "Make me a Cuba Libre, would you, Henry?"

"I'm sorry," Henry said. "I don't know how."

"Rum and Coke, for God's sake."

"Rum and . . . ?"

"I'll make it."

Bewildering, all those bottles. And the noise. And the people. Where the hell could they all have come from? "I'm afraid I'm not much of a one for parties."

"I'm glad you told me that. I should never have guessed."

Under the Gibralfaro, the Calle del Principe. White walls and the cobbled street, dappled in the starlight. The heavy nocturnal silence of the south. The shadows of palm fronds, motionless; no wind, no breeze at all.

Number 42 was a house like any of the others on the long slope, but had in place of a dark front window a wide panel of reinforced glass, an *escaparate*, behind which was piled a random array of sun creams, liver pills, weird cosmetic appliances and cheap sun-glasses; above the panel, in cracked red paint, was the barely legible sign FARMACIA PEDRES. To the right was the high iron screen to the front door. It stood unlatched, a little ajar.

Behind the front door was a small room, floored with dingy grey tiles. There was a high serving counter and an old-fashioned till; the till was locked, and didn't look worth the trouble of opening. A door behind the counter led into the store-room and from there a staircase mounted to the first floor; alternatively, you could go through another wooden door and pass into the central patio, which was small and hung with creepers and smelt deep and musty, like a cell. There was room there for a large table and for three or four wicker chairs; in one of the chairs Cipriano sat, his feet pushed out in front of him, his hands in his pockets. He sat in near-darkness; a tiny 25-watt bulb in a wall socket high overhead did very little to dissipate the gloom, but served chiefly to attract a seething commotion of small flies and moths; from time to time Cipriano took a hand from one pocket and swatted at his face and neck, calmly, methodically, yet abstractedly. His jacket hung on the back of his chair and he had loosened his tie. From behind the half-shuttered room to his left there came an occasional clink of heavy china and a smell of slowly-percolating coffee. Cipriano had never been to this house before, but he felt very much at home.

He didn't look round when Ramona came back into the patio, shuffling on slippered feet and carrying the coffee-tray. "Nothing like good coffee," he said sententiously. "Without sugar. There's nothing better. *Creo yo.*"

Ramona said nothing. She put the two well-filled cups down on the table and then sat down opposite him; he saw that her hands were still white and delicate. She'd put on weight since they'd last met, but in the right places. She balanced well. "How long have you been here? In this place?"

"Nearly six months now."

"You like it?"

"No."

A silly question. This was Malaga. Ramona came from Sevilla. "The neighbours?"

"They're cows. We don't get on."

She sat well forward in her chair, her arms emerging startlingly white from the short sleeves of the black cotton housecoat, moving against the dark filigree shadows of the wall creepers. China clinked again as she stirred her coffee. She'd be pushing forty, he thought; but in the half-light, she didn't look it. "A chemist's shop. That's new."

"It's been here for years, they tell me."

"I meant, new for *you*."

"One shop is very like another."

"I suppose so. Who runs it for you?"

"I run it."

The voice, dry and laconic. Economical in the use of words as of anything else; generations of village poverty underlying it. "Who mixes the prescriptions? Does that kind of thing?"

"You saw him. That bloke who was working here. Pedrito. He came with the shop."

"Ah," Cipriano said. He tried the coffee, which was boiling hot.

"If what you mean is, am I getting it regular, then the answer's mind your own bloody business."

"*Qué cosas tienes,*" Cipriano said.

"I know you."

"Of old."

"Yes," Ramona said. "Of old." And laughed, and suddenly looked even younger. She was, Cipriano thought, a remarkable woman.

"Ramona?"

"Yes?"

"It's good to see you again."

40

"Yes," she said. She took her hand from the coffee-cup and touched the back of his, briefly, with the tips of her fingers. It wasn't a sentimental gesture; it was simply an acknowledgement. They were both there. Both still alive. "You're bringing trouble. I know that. But even so, I'm glad to see you."

"There's a message from Martin."

"Yes. Or you wouldn't be here."

"Our information is accurate. And you're to take action."

"Yes." She sighed. "Trouble. There you are."

"Hernandez?"

"Yes. It's Hernandez."

Yes, yes, yes, all along the line. Except to the one thing that was always no. And about that, she was probably right as well. Cipriano sipped at his coffee, his eyes half-closed in appreciative meditation. "He's coming to Malaga, then."

"Torrevedra. On the twenty-seventh."

"Do we know what for?"

"Some kind of a deal he has on with Martorell. Does it matter?"

"No," Cipriano said. "... He's clever, Martin is. How did Martin know?"

"A year ago, it had to be a guess. That's the thing about guesses. Some of them come off. Others don't."

"Even so, it won't be all that easy."

"They want the two of them," Ramona said.

"The *two* of them?"

"Hernandez. And Martorell. Both. There'll be papers involved. Documents. The documents have to be destroyed."

"A bomb job, then."

"It looks like that. A bomb. And with no mistakes."

Farmacia Pedres, Cipriano thought. *A chemist's shop. That's new.* I was slow, there. I should have guessed. But, God, home-made explosives. That's no kind of a joke.

"There's two of them and two of you. That makes the odds even."

41

There'd been that place in Madrid, off the Calle del Gato. Five years back, or was it more? ... with the jelly in plastic bottles, a nice little turnover. The stuff going off in railway stations, restaurants, government offices, all over Madrid; it had got into all the papers that winter. Not even the censors had been able to hold it up. Then suddenly, the house had turned into a pile of blackened brick and timber under a wreath of smoke. No one knew how it had happened; it had been weeks before they'd even found out exactly who was killed. Seven, was the conclusion they'd come to. Seven at a blow. All good workmen. Martin and the others had rather gone off jelly after that. No wonder. It was very nasty stuff.

Two of them, two of you. The words taking some time to sink in. "The English boy, you mean?"

"He knows about bombs."

"I doubt if he knows much about anything else. He's very young."

"*How* young?"

"I don't know. It's hard to tell, with foreigners. I'd say nineteen or twenty ... A boy, anyway."

"Then maybe *you*'re getting it regular," Ramona said. This was very funny and she laughed very loudly for several seconds, long snorting near-masculine peals that involved her whole body from the hips up, while Cipriano smiled quietly, politely. It was nice to see Ramona in good humour. "No," he said. "I've formed my habits. And I'm too old to change."

"Plenty of scope for them, at Torrevedra."

"A great deal to look at. But not much to touch."

"Expensive, yes. They would be."

"Well, no. If they do it at all, they'll do it for free. But the trouble is they *know* nothing. They have no real idea what it's all about. Maybe they are looking, but they're looking in all the wrong places. It's very sad."

"Sad for you, yes," Ramona said. "You old goat."

Henry had never been up in Santiago's flat before. He'd certainly never realised the true extent of the view it commanded. There were wide French windows that gave on to a narrow balcony, and from there by day the view must have been spectacular; by night it was little less so, with the overhead orange lights of the Torrevedra road network imposing a scrawled pattern on the dark rock wilderness and with those of the big office block, some two hundred yards distant from him but far beneath, illuminating the lawn, the hotel gardens, the patches of palm and yucca. Behind the office and reaching up to the hills, the houses, the villas, the bungalows; squares, rectangles and arches of dimmer light; and nearer at hand the bright flickering radiance of an open-air cinema, Rock Hudson and Doris Day cavorting to a well-filled last house.

Then the main road to Malaga, silver headlights racing their black shadows one after another down the straight stretch to Los Boliches, with a whisper of sound from the thrumming motors carried up by the slow sea breeze; and behind the road the sea itself, black, unmoving, its horizon just discernible against a pale night sky and the bright lights of the fishing boats punctuating its velvet surface. Then the stars. The burning stars, thousands upon thousands. A perfect and uncluttered view from a height of twelve storeys round an arc of some two hundred and forty degrees; only the mountain was hidden from view by the low white wall of the penthouse. The mountain, and the mountain top. No windows looked out in that direction. The cold would come drifting down from there in the late winter, but wouldn't penetrate.

It wasn't cold tonight. It was hot, in spite of the sea breeze; inside the penthouse flat, it was very hot. There was a big room, a very big room, behind the french windows

43

and the plate glass; it was difficult, at first glance, to see how big because it was L-shaped, because the lights were very low and because in the farther wing of the L—where Santi's guests were dancing to taped music—the hotel electricians had arranged some weird kaleidoscopic effects; the sort of lighting system that Henry, ill-versed in these matters, associated with so-called Happenings in London strip clubs. It made it not merely difficult to assess the size of the room, but difficult to make out with any clarity the outlines of one's dancing partner three feet away; no doubt this was precisely the effect desired. Henry guessed, anyway, that Santiago's flat would have accommodated with ease his own little cubby-hole and twelve others like it. He didn't resent this, of course. He simply noted it.

A big room, but hot; very hot. There were too many people for the air conditioning to cope with; too much expensive perfume, too much cigar smoke, too much—to be vulgar—sweat. And a lot of the people, especially the women, had taken a lot of their clothes off. Very sensible, of course. They probably felt more comfortable that way. But Henry didn't. It was possible that he had unconsciously chosen to study the room and its varied appointments in order to distract his attention from the occupants, Santi's guests, and from what they were doing. It wasn't that he felt out of place, exactly. He'd felt that way at first, talking to Anita. But once Anita had left him—had moved away from the bar, glass in hand, to disappear he didn't know where—nobody had taken any further notice of him whatsoever.

Ghosts don't feel out of place. Henry felt like a ghost. No one as yet had actually tried to walk straight through him, but Henry's sense of his own intangibility was becoming such as to lead him to believe that, had anyone tried to do it, the attempt might well have succeeded. It wasn't that people hadn't spoken to him. Quite a few people—people that, in the outside world, he knew—had spoken to him, but not as though he were in any true sense *there*. He stood beside small groups of people holding hair-raisingly intimate conversations; they included him in the group without giving him a glance, and the effect of this, paradoxically, was to exclude him utterly. It was weird. Quite unreal. For someone who normally didn't drink, it was true that he'd drunk a good deal; but no, it wasn't that. It was the people. They were extraordinary.

Petrie, for instance. He'd been normal enough that morning. And normal enough when he'd come into the hotel a couple of hours ago—normal for an Englishman, anyway. The distant but courteous nod, the dissociated smile; just right for recognising, on foreign soil, the existence of a fellow-countryman of inferior financial status. Now here he was on a green velvet sofa, a lit wax candle in one hand and what looked like a fifteen-year-old girl in, or rather under, the other. Unfocused eyes. A pally grin. "You know me? I'm Michael. Michael."

"Yes. Hullo." Henry, uncertain.

And to the girl, "You don't know me, do you? I'm Michael. Michael Faraday." She went on staring past Henry's right shoulder with large and serious eyes. There was a thread of saliva running down her chin. "I'm about to give a lecture to the Royal Society."

His diction was perfectly clear. So he couldn't be drunk, surely? ". . . What about?"

"What about? About what? About candles, mate."

"Oh," Henry said.

"Candle. You see? Candle."

He took his right hand from the girl's bare thigh to approach it slowly, from above, to the candle flame. "Umbra. Penumbra." His palm entering the flame, pressing it downwards. He held his hand there, unmoving, for several seconds; his eyes watching the flame, studying it closely. No sign of pain.

45

"God," Henry said. "Doesn't it . . . ?"

No. It seemed it didn't. The girl was also watching closely now; no sign of surprise. And Henry, seriously perplexed, had moved on towards the french windows. Fresh air was what he wanted. To reach the balcony, he had to step over another very young girl, lying on the floor; not passed out, but seemingly deep in thought. She was moving her tongue constantly, restlessly, over her lips. She wore a bright yellow dress with a large hole over the midriff; someone—conceivably she herself—had drawn a circle with lipstick around her navel. "Excuse me," Henry said. She ignored him totally.

Then the balcony, the night, the sea and the stars.

I'm not, he thought, leaning on the parapet, much of a one for parties. So what am I doing here? Lurching about as though on the edge of a mystery. There's no mystery here. Just the usual noisy preludes to middle-class promiscuity, guitars on tape and women screaming; just the brief adultery rituals of the Spanish summer. Rituals are for the initiated. And I don't belong. What's so perplexing about that?'

I can see it all from outside. Looking back through the windows from here on the balcony. The lurid multi-coloured lights glowing on the dance floor, the darkness over the corner couches where the wall lamps had been switched off. Switch off and switch on. Cannabis, would it be? Or L.S.D.? One of those things. It can't be in the drink, though. *I've* been drinking. I've drunk too much. Here on the balcony I can feel the dampness inside my shirt, under my belt. I'll catch pneumonia. That girl on the floor by the window, she was wearing next to nothing. Just the dress with the hole in it. You could see her breasts. She'd get pneumonia for sure. Lying there by the door. I ought to go and . . . But if I touched her . . .

Oh *God*, Henry thought.

46

He leaned farther out over the parapet and was, in no way to his surprise, sick.

"You don't like it, do you?"

"No."

"Why not?"

"Bombs are tricky things."

"Not for experts."

"Bombs are tricky things even for experts."

"I'll have to see him."

"Henry?"

"Yes."

"I'll bring him."

"They say he knows all about bombs. But..."

"You'd like to form your own opinion."

"Yes."

The coffee was long since finished. Ramona had drawn back the canvas *toldo* that roofed the patio during the day, and now overhead in a square of sky the bunched stars prickled. "And I need more things," she said. "More information."

"Such as?"

"A good map. Or an air photograph. Up to date. The route will have to be worked out. We'll do that together."

"We haven't much time before the twenty-seventh."

"The ones where you have to wait ... they're the worst."

"I suppose so. Yes, that's true. These days I tire easily."

"Don't start off on that again," Ramona said.

"It's not just a matter of age. It's like going to the bank. You start off with just so much money; you go to the bank time and again and there's always something there. Until one day there isn't. That can happen to you at any age, but one day, sooner or later, it has to happen." A pause; then the red glow of his cigarette-end in the near-darkness, the still air tinged for a second with the smell of black tobacco.

"They don't send you a statement, is the trouble. You've no way at all of knowing when."

"Banks," Ramona said. "They're for capitalists."

"It's a way of putting it."

"They'd tell you what to do all right. You put more money in. That's the answer."

"That's not possible."

"That's why they send these young ones. They've got money to spare. They can lend us some."

Cipriano said nothing but, in the near-darkness, shook his head.

"You're not happy about him, are you? *El inglesito?*"

"I don't know," Cipriano said. "I expect he's brave enough. They usually are. It isn't exactly bravery, what I'm talking about."

"What, then?"

"Willpower, perhaps. Something like that."

". . . Whatever it is," Ramona said, dismissing it with an impatient lift of her shoulders. She leaned forwards to collect the coffee cups, to put them back on the tray.

"And you? Don't *you* think about these things?"

"Women don't think."

"True. They don't. Yes. That's perfectly true." His gaze, turned casually towards the low vee of her housecoat as it deepened to her stoop, became abstracted, as if this were some new philosophical idea of far-reaching import. "Women *last* better than men do. Mentally. Physically. In every way. And that's what I notice about the boy. He doesn't think, either."

"So much the better," Ramona said. Her chair squeaked back on the patio floor. She stood up.

"Ramona, *sabes algo?*"

"*Qué?*"

". . . I don't *have* to go back tonight."

"Yes, you do."

Facing him, the tray held at hip-level. Under the house-

48

coat strong legs, good legs, dancer's legs; she still moved easily, gracefully, with that innate sense of bodily balance that the blondes in the bikinis lacked. Cipriano nodded, reaching back to hook his thumb in the loop at the collar of his jacket. "Is anything the matter?"

"There doesn't have to be anything the matter. *Que no tengo ganas.* That's all."

When he had gone, she locked and bolted the iron screen behind him and then the shop door. It was well after midnight. And it was true that she felt tired.

Moving past the counter on her way back to the stairs, she stopped beside the weighing machine and stared into the flyblown mirror that hung just above it. The face beneath the mop of heavy black hair seemed more sharply-contoured than usual; the pale, shiny skin was drawn back from the cheekbones, deepening the crows'-feet at the corners of her eyes. It was a narrow face, triangular, fox-like, and the eyes too were like those of an animal; lustrous, wary, yet curiously innocent eyes that looked out on herself as from the depths of a dark burrow. Women don't think. They watch, they assess, they react intuitively.

No. There was nothing the matter. It was just that she didn't like it when people talked that way; about courage, willpower, going to the bank, all that nonsense. She didn't like abstractions. She was not particularly afraid of death; that was an abstraction like any other. But she was afraid of growing old. That was real. The creases in the skin, the sagging flesh. It was stupid, perhaps, to have said no. Cipriano was a man, had been looking at her as a woman. And men wouldn't do that always.

She'd put on weight these last six months, here in the languid heat of Malaga. But then you don't expect to stay slim, once you're past thirty-five. She pulled the loose belt of the housecoat downwards, and the thin black cotton

49

tightened over the bulk of her breasts; too heavy, no doubt about it, but at least keeping their shape. She saw a bead of sweat on her upper lip and wiped it away with a piece of paper tissue, taken from her pocket.

Anyway, no need to worry. She wouldn't get to be old. She turned the key to the light switch and padded through the empty darkness towards the stairs. To hell with men, all men, and especially to hell with Martin. Cipriano, as usual, had done all the complaining, but she didn't like this job, either. She didn't like it at all.

After the bout of sickness the lights, the swimming lights, slowly took on focus and pattern until at last they conformed to reality; Henry stood with his elbows on the parapet, aware again of the strange coldness of the moisture on his forehead, of the sharp burning pain at the pit of his stomach. He stood motionless in the shadows, head lowered, enjoying the unutterable pleasure of not, for the time being, having to spew; he had also a feeling of vertigo that wasn't so pleasant. That was why he stood so still. After a while he heard Anita's voice, low-pitched, like an echo to the beating in his ears. He didn't catch what she'd said but it didn't matter; he'd probably invented it. But then came the other voice, equally lowpitched but real, not blending with Henry's thoughts but disturbing them.

". . . For them as likes views . . ."

And, unmistakably, Anita's giggle. Henry, lifting and turning his head with some little difficulty, saw them as a single blurred figure at the end of the balcony, some five long paces away. "No, look. *Why* won't you?"

"Oh, just because."

"I meant it, you know. What I said."

"You always want to rush things."

"Of course I do. So would you—if you were me."

There were roses somewhere. Henry could smell them.

And that pervading drift of cigar-smoke. The sickness had moved back to his stomach again; oh no, he thought. God, no. Not now.

"And that Petrie girl?"

"What about her?"

"Rushing things a bit there too, aren't you?"

"I have to chat the girls up at parties—you know that."

"I can't imagine why you ask half these people. They could get you into trouble, couldn't they?"

"I don't see how. I don't give them the stuff."

"It's your place. Your party."

"So what? It's none of my business. Live and let live, that's my motto. And anyway, there's a lot of us left who prefer the old-fashioned alcohol. *You're* not drinking."

"Not right now."

"Come on. Drink."

"I'm just—"

"*Drink.*"

"Oh God." Peripheral vision, was that the trick of it? Looking half away, you saw them better, though even then not clearly; they stood very close together. Santi seemed to have one hand at the back of her neck, tilting her head; with the other he held a full tumbler to her mouth. Then, predictably enough, a coughing splutter. "Hey, hey," Santiago said. And Henry, taking his chance, moved away; went back through the open door, stepping again over the prostrate body of the girl who again ignored him. Henry had decided he'd had enough. He was going home.

At the far end of the hot room, where the lights were strongest, more dazzling, more confusing, each of the dancers moved in a private world of coloured splinters and revolving mirror-images. The walls were outer darkness, empty space, non-existent; the shifting filter-lenses were the centre of all being, creating a fog of radiance through which poured loudly and incessantly the raucous, pulsing beat of the pop groups and a tropical, an over-

51

whelming heat. A pallid green face swung towards Henry, blotched abruptly with bruised purple as fingers clutched startlingly at his shirt-front; a mouth came open, said something quite inaudible. "No, thank you," Henry said. The face, barred and flecked now with blue as though seen through drifting weeds at the bottom of the ocean, turned and swam away; the blue-and-green body beneath it seemed to be completely naked. Surely not, though, thought Henry. There'd be tights or something. He moved out of the echoing sea and into the darkness, found the exit door and pushed it open. Outside was the carpeted corridor, the waiting lift; closing the door, the silence was instantly complete. The flat was sound-proofed, obviously. No wonder. Had it been real? Had *any* of it been real?

That half-choking, half-giggling splutter. The two dimly-seen figures at the parapet. Odd, how his mind retained that sound, that image. And the dancers moving barefoot with an awkward, spasmodic tread.

2

Gomez believed it, anyway, and appeared to be suitably impressed. "You've got a cheek, I'll say that for you. Just walking in on him like that. *I* wouldn't have had the nerve."

"I told you. Anita took me up."

"She only works here. Same as you and me. And she'll be out on her ear, what's more, as soon as Santi-boy's had what he wants. So she'd better play it cool if she has any sense. It's all happened before."

"Oh, she'll play it cool all right," Henry said.

It all seemed very dull and ordinary, this morning. Anita was a very stupid girl, and he couldn't personally care much less if she played it cool or not. You'd have thought that Santiago would know how very stupid she was; but maybe womanisers—and this was Henry's private suspicion —don't as a rule know very much about women, anyway. To hell with them both, he felt. They deserved one another.

"He'll have a brute of a hangover," Gomez said, with satisfaction.

"Who?"

"*El jefe*. He hasn't come in yet this morning. Not that there's anything at all unusual about *that*."

"I'll tell you something else," Henry said.

"What?"

"You can see right into the office from that front room of his. You can see everything that's going on. He could probably see us two right now, with a good pair of field-glasses."

Gomez started to turn his head, then checked himself.

"You think that's what he does?"

"It wouldn't surprise me."

"No. Nor me, either. *Demonios*." Looking back, this time as though casually, to peer up at the concrete and plate-glass cliff of the hotel behind the office lawn. "My God, you're right. That's taking the Big Brother angle a bit too bloody far, if you ask me."

"I don't suppose he bothers."

"Not with us, no. Why should he? The typists next door, they'd be more in his line. His private harem." Gomez snuffled sardonically in his moustache and, picking up a pen, commenced to initial papers. "That drug stuff, though. He'll have to be careful. We had some trouble with that a year or so back—the Civis poking round. Just the kind of thing we don't want."

"Bad publicity," Henry said.

"Well, of course. People come here to relax; they don't like having wagonloads of busies turning their houses inside out. It may be all right for that lot of shit you get over in Torre, but not for *our* lot. They don't want to know. And they're rich enough to think they don't have to stand for it."

"I suppose we do have a certain amount of pull."

"At the Comisaria? ... The Old Man certainly does. Old Martorell. Oh, our lot can get away with just about anything in the way of drink and sex and ... bikinis, and all that jazz ... That's what the place is *for*, isn't it? If the foreigners couldn't get it here, they'd damned soon move off somewhere else. But not drugs. No. Not drugs. We're too near Morocco for that to be a joke."

The telephone was ringing. He picked it up, listened for a moment; then held it out to Henry.

"It's for you."

The appointment was at the La Perla bar in Fuengirola,

during the lunch hour. Cipriano was waiting when Henry arrived. There he contrived, in the space of ten minutes, to set Henry's world upside down all over again.

"... And you want us to go there tonight?"

"She wants to see you," Cipriano said patiently.

"All right. I'll be there. Nine o'clock?"

"Nine o'clock."

Sitting outside La Perla, you could see the hills of Torrevedra in the distance. The hills and the mountain. And the square block of the hotel at something under two miles' distance. It looked completely different, that morning. That's what knowledge does. It changes things.

It would be Martorell—someone who was something other than just a name. Santi's father. That morning, he and Gomez had been laughing, joking, in their usual uneasy alliance; Santiago, as always, in part a figure of fun, in part their common enemy. Now he was, by virtue of his connection with destiny, with incipient death, in a way made real—sanctified; knowledge of this kind was like a sudden gift of second sight, enabling one to see into the heart of things. Enmity, envy had disappeared; in their place, a certain compassion.

Compassion without pity.

For this, after all, is the ultimate power. To know exactly when someone is going to die. The gift of grace, so long awaited, had come, and was every bit as exciting as Henry had supposed.

"She'll want photographs," Cipriano said.

Henry looked at the camera in its leather case, slung from the arm of Cipriano's chair. "Who of?"

"Of Santiago's office. Inside and out. Can you manage that?"

"I know how a camera works," Henry said. "If that's what you mean."

"If you can do it this afternoon, you won't need a flash. The meter's pre-set for indoor shots. No problem, then?"

"No," Henry said. "No problem."

Cipriano hadn't expected him to take it all so calmly. Cipriano had expected questions, comments; difficulties, in short. It was all very puzzling. But then, he didn't understand the English.

He could see Henry's white shirt pinkish-black in the glow of the red overhead bulb, and he could see Henry's face, or part of it, in profile, deeply shadowed. If by daylight that face seemed to him unexpressive, the soft red glow petrified it, froze it to utter stillness; it could have been the face of a corpse. Nothing of what Ramona was saying seemed to register upon it in the slightest; but for an occasional nod, you'd have said that Henry wasn't understanding a word. An effect of the light, though, surely. It had to be.

"We don't know exactly when they'll arrive," Ramona said. "But later, we'll be told. Meanwhile we can take it they'll be arriving separately at the office—by car, of course. Martorell first. Then Hernandez."

"We want them both," Cipriano said; and afterwards, wondered why he'd spoken. In the hope, maybe, of securing some kind of a reaction—a turn of the head—anything. But Henry remained impassive. And Ramona:

"They'll go into Santiago Martorell's private office and there'll be some kind of a discussion. No one else will be present—that's almost certain. And at the end of the discussion, documents will be signed. Contracts. We want those contracts destroyed. So now you see why it has to be a bomb."

This the key-word, triggering off in Henry an instant response. "An incendiary, then."

"Yes, but we also want Martorell and Hernandez put out of the way. An incendiary by itself—that mightn't do the trick. There must be high explosive, also, A dual-purpose

56

bomb. This," Ramona said, "is why we need an expert."

"Most incendiaries are explosive," Henry said. "And most explosives burn. It's a matter of how the energy's released. It doesn't sound like too much of a problem."

"Good. But you'll realise we've no direct source of supply. Whatever it is we use, we must make it ourselves. *You* will have to make it. I can help."

She could see now, lowering her head, the first glimmer of grey in the darkness of the developing tray. The liquid swirled silently as she moved it. In the small darkroom, it was stiflingly hot; there were drops of sweat on her forehead. "I was trained once as a chemist. Many years ago ... I know that medicines are one thing and high explosives another. But you'll find I'm careful. And I have steady hands."

Henry had reverted to silence. But now his head moved, a very little, watching her lift the print from the tray—a ten-inch square of smooth, dripping paper—and move across to clip it to the drying board. "*Ya está!* That's the last. These are good photographs, Henry."

Cipriano said, "You haven't fixed them."

"No. I'll destroy them as soon as we've examined them together. And the negatives, too. I told you ... I am careful."

"Shall I turn on the light?"

"Yes. And open the door, I could do with some fresh air. Or what passes for fresh air, in this bloody town." A pause as Cipriano turned the light switch and a harder, brighter light irradiated them. "Do you come to Malaga often, Henry?"

Henry's eyelids were lowered against the narrowing of his pupils; he regretted, rather, the loss of the red bulb's dimness, its flow of intimacy. "Well, no. Not very often." Ramona was watching him without any hint of a smile, yet he sensed, somehow, that she found him mildly amusing; rather as did Anita, yet in a different way. He couldn't

57

put it more exactly than that—how do you describe amusement?—but he found it annoying. Annoying, though, precisely because it was indefinable. He was impressed with Ramona. She was careful, all right, and he liked careful people; but there was more to it than that. She had serenity; an inner calmness that seemed an animal, rather than a human, quality. Animals don't get worried. Nor did Ramona. Talking to her was like talking to a very intelligent dog; it was relaxing. But also odd, of course, because she wasn't a dog.

"Not very often. That's right. You're careful, too. I like a man who doesn't commit himself." She tapped the clipped-up prints lightly with one fingertip. "Yes. These are good photographs. They'll take a whole lot more enlarging, if it's necessary. But I don't think it will be. Cipriano?"

Cipriano, coming across from the opened door. There were four photographs; Martorell's office, viewed from four different angles. He leaned forwards to study each of them in turn, then nodded in agreement.

"Very good. Very clear."

"These papers," Henry said abruptly. "Are they in the safe?"

"No. Hernandez will be bringing them. In a brief-case, I would imagine."

"The way we see it," Cipriano said, "Martorell will get there first. Probably, he won't go into the office right away. He'll wait for Hernandez to arrive. Then when Hernandez comes, they'll go in together. It seems reasonable to suppose that when they do, Martorell will sit behind the desk. And Hernandez will then take *this* chair—it seems a safe bet." Taking a pencil from his breast pocket to point at the nearest print. "Right here. Facing him. The question is what he'd then do with the brief-case. The natural thing to do would be either to put it down on the floor ... here

58

to the right of the chair, he's right-handed ... or else just to put it on top of the desk."

"It makes a difference," Henry said.

"Yes, it does. If it's on the floor, it'll be in this angle between the chair and the desk and it'll be pretty well protected. The thing is that sooner or later the papers'll be taken out—they've got to be signed—and that's when they'll be vulnerable. The trouble is that we don't know how long the usual polite chitchat is going to last. So we—"

"It won't last for long," Ramona said. "They're busy men. Time is money. Five minutes at the most."

"Say five minutes, then. From the time they enter the room. But..." Cipriano rubbed his chin. "It's tricky."

"Time mechanisms aren't that accurate. Not the kind that we could fix for ourselves, anyway. And we'd have to set it a good few hours before."

"We're not thinking of time mechanisms, Henry. At least, not exactly."

"A grenade, then?"

"God, no. We're not going to walk up and chuck the thing through the window, you know. We have *some* instincts of self-preservation, and so for that matter has Martorell. He'll have his Security crowd with him and plenty of them."

"It'll still have to be a fairish size," Henry said. "You won't get the effect you want with a thing like a cigarette packet. So if it's not a grenade, where are we going to *hide* it?"

"We've a plan for that, as far as it goes." Ramona was sitting now on the work-bench, plimsolled feet dangling, her hands resting squarely on her knees; an awkward but a surprisingly youthful pose. "We just had to be sure that the idea would work. That's why we needed the photographs." The light bulb directly over her head accentuated the deep shadows under her eyes, the puffiness of her cheeks; her pale calm middle-aged face seemed almost violently

59

at odds with her posture. "Where would you say was the ideal place for it, Henry?"

"Inside the desk, I suppose. The top drawer, maybe. But if the Security people go through the place first ..." Henry shrugged. "And the drawers are steel-lined. Fire precautions. No, ideally, you'd want two charges. One under each chair. But again, they'd be bound to find them if they looked."

"They'll look," Ramona said. "People have gone after Martorell before. They'll look very carefully."

"Then it's difficult. Like I said—it can't be *too* small."

"Suppose we had something on top of the desk. How would that be, from your point of view?"

"A cigar-box? Something like that?"

"Yes, something very like that."

"Grand."

"Yes. Without being experts," Ramona said, "that was what we'd thought."

"But that's much too chancey. I mean, all these things you see on top of the desk ... that's Santiago's stuff. That's why it's such a mess. He's not very tidy. Well, they're bound to clear things up a bit before the meeting. All those correspondence trays ... Just about the lot. Wouldn't you say?"

"Not everything." Cipriano, still standing by the prints and peering at them now more closely than ever.

"No?"

"No. What about this?"

He reached out, dabbed with the pencil again. Henry stooped forwards. Then straightened again, rubbing the back of his head.

"I see what you mean."

"We could get half a kilo of jelly into the base, if we packed it carefully. Would that do the trick?"

"It'd be strange," Henry said, "if it didn't."

"Well, I'm an expert, too, don't forget."

Henry's mood of impassivity seemed to be on the verge of breaking, Cipriano thought. He was almost—not quite, but almost—smiling.

"Something goes wrong, you see, the day before. I'm called in to fix it, so I go round in the evening ... and I fix it. That's all there is to it. It's sweet. And we don't need a timing mechanism, that's the real beauty of it. We fire the detonator from the trembler, or we could have a plunger to make the contact when it rings and someone picks it up. Of course it can be packed with jelly and still work."

"All you need is the current from the cable."

"And the connection to be made. That's all."

"By dialling the number?"

"On automatic."

"My God," Henry said. "You could do it from bloody Madrid, then. If you wanted to."

"Long-range execution, you might call it. Assassination by telephone. And it's going to worry them a good deal, you know, because the chances are they won't be able to work out right away exactly how we did it."

"Who thought of it? Was it you?"

"I first suggested it a couple of years ago. But the idea's nothing. Planning to use it—that's what takes the brains and the patience. Getting us three together, all at the right time, at the right place. Too many good ideas are wasted, you know, in this business. But this idea won't be."

A draught of cooler air came in through the door, ruffling Henry's hair where his hand had lifted it. And Ramona swung her feet down from the work-bench, touching him on the arm as she moved past. "Let's go into the patio. It's getting too hot in here. And the coffee should be ready."

In the patio the portable radio stood on the table, transistorising into the near-darkness a soft, muted howl of flamenco. Cipriano turned the volume control down, then sat heavily in the chair that he had occupied the previous night. Henry took the rocking-chair in the near corner; it squeaked gently in cross-rhythm to the music as he pushed it to and fro. It wasn't a nervous movement; he had, and knew that he had, himself under excellent control. But the internal excitement continued to simmer, as within the strung muscles of a racing driver; he was even conscious of a slight pain in his diaphragm, as though the ligaments there had been over-tautened, and rocking the chair, he found, eased that small pain a very little. His mouth seemed more than ordinarily dry. He was looking forward to the coffee.

"Did you do the installations?"

"No. But I've checked them."

". . . Because I noticed there were two. Telephones."

"That's right. And if I were an amateur I'd have to be very careful to get the right one, because one of them runs on a closed line. To Santiago's flat. He had that one put in for obvious reasons. But the other one's open. Fuengirola 324 and ask for Fifi." His hands opened and closed in a little involuntary gesture, difficult to interpret. "I'm not an amateur, though. And there won't be any mistakes of *that* kind. Don't worry."

"These Security people," Henry said. "Mightn't they check the 'phones to see if they're tapped?"

"If they do, they'll only unscrew the mouthpieces. And everything'll be in order. If you want to hide something, you know, it's not a bad idea to tuck it inside something that's an object of suspicion already—for a different reason. People's minds move in familiar paths. You see a telephone and you think, Ah!—better make sure it isn't bugged. You don't think—better make sure it isn't a bomb. The Security boys are usually very thorough—private or State Security, it makes no difference. But they stick to routine. If you break routine, you've a chance of getting through—and in this case, a good one. The only doubt I have is about the explosive. I mean, this handmade stuff is pretty unstable."

"Very."

"It wouldn't go off, though, if you just moved the telephone a little?"

"Not if it was properly packed. It would if you dropped it."

"That's a million-to-one chance. People think of telephones as delicate instruments, which up to a point of course they are. Once in a while you might drop the receiver, but you practically never drop the whole damned thing. Yes, that's a chance we can reasonably take."

There was movement in the shadows by the doorway; Ramona, bringing in the coffee-tray again. "Have you tried it out?" Henry asked.

"It's never been done before, as far as I know. Certainly not by any of us."

"No, I meant just tried out. To see if it works."

"I can't see any reason why it shouldn't work."

"Oh, nor can I. But then there are lots of things that ought to work. And don't."

"You think we ought to have a dummy run?"

"Yes, just try it out somewhere. Then if there *are* any snags to it, we'll find them."

"A careful man," Ramona said, putting down the tray. "I like that. And I agree with you."

"It's a matter of the time factor," Cipriano said. "We'd have to do it soon. Very soon. Otherwise, it shouldn't be too hard to arrange. There are plenty of places up in the hills where..." He looked up at Henry. "How long does it take to make the jelly?"

"Not long. Today's Friday. We could make some tomorrow night—if the shop's clear then."

"The shop will be clear," Ramona said, "whenever you want it." Then a little hurriedly, as if to correct some misleading impression that the phrase might have left— "We don't do what you'd call a roaring trade, at the best of times."

"Then I'll try," Cipriano said, "to fix up something for Sunday."

Ramona picked up the *cafetera* and trickled coffee into deep cups. On the table, the radio went on whining to itself against a rattling guitar. Henry closed his eyes for a moment. He felt tired.

Later on, back in his room again, he wondered what he'd made all the fuss about.

Of course the thing would work. Impulse detonation, there was nothing simpler. He could remember the copper cable unwound from the reel and strung the full length of the workshed, his father's blunt, strong fingers plugging the leads in to the terminal. Then, behind the wire cage and the mica plate, the sharp, bright stab of flame. And the sealed can circled, as neatly as with a tin-opener; its shape still perfect, the thin sides not even dented; his own small fingers, running round the inside of the rim, finding only smooth metal. Then he had done the same—packed the charge, prepared the wiring, made the connection— to the same result; the tin sheared at the seam, not even a roughness where it had split. "That's a good trick, Dad."

"Takes the line of maximum resistance. Like I told you."

Nodding in satisfaction; the shadow of the sharp peak of his cap dancing over his eyes and wrinkled forehead. The tight mouth temporarily relaxed.

"...Not really a trick, though. Don't start to think of it in that way."

"I was only—"

"Explosives aren't for tricks. For being clever. Remember that, boy. Don't you ever forget it."

The shape of the tin still perfect. But the metal hot to

64

the touch. Henry hadn't forgotten.

Was that where the trouble lay? In the idea being that little bit too clever...? But then it wasn't a trick, it was anything but a trick. At the end of it, two people would be dead. *That* was what explosives were for.

So why be difficult? Why the dummy run?

It wasn't necessary. Perhaps he could still call it off. This whole operation had been worked out with care, that much was obvious. They'd been expecting this meeting for some time past—perhaps for months; and they'd prepared the ingredients of the attack as meticulously as if they'd been making the gelignite itself. They needed one electronic engineer, one chemist, one explosives expert; all at the right place at the right time, and all with unexceptionable motives for being there. Each one of the team with a part to play; each one necessary. A real computer-planned job. And he'd been thinking—insofar as he'd done any thinking at all—in terms of chucking grenades through windows and running like hell. It was embarrassing, in a way. Martin and his people weren't amateurs. They'd spent their lives thinking, planning, computing. In the long run, they'd win. It was inevitable.

All the same—he was getting to it now—it was what he hadn't liked, and still didn't; being a pawn in a complex gambit, playing a part in an elaborately preconceived plan. That had to be why he'd tried to stick his heels in—just to show he had a mind of his own. And that, too, had been pretty stupid, really. Childish. They hadn't been impressed; he knew that.

If people really *knew* (you said to yourself), then they'd be impressed. *Who? Henry? Never! I can't believe it...* An expert, not all that many people are experts. Not for tricks, no, never for tricks. But for the real thing. But Cipriano knew, and now this Ramona woman, and they weren't impressed, and there wasn't any reason why they should be. They were experts, too. They'd killed people already. It was really a different Henry who had thought that way (Henry thought, almost asleep). When the job was done, and done neatly, they'd accept the new Henry as an equal and the others, the ones who didn't know, they just didn't count. Their admiration wasn't worth having. After all, if you killed people...

Tap. Tap. Tap.

(His head jerking sideways on the pillow.)

Silence.

Then *tap, tap* again.

He rolled off the bed, went to unlock and open the door. Anita.

"Oh. It's you."

"Can I come in?"

She stepped past without looking at him, sat down in the narrow chair. "I tried once before. But you weren't in."

"I was out."

"That's right. You were out. You weren't in. I wanted to talk to you."

Henry looked at his wrist-watch. A quarter to one. "Would you like some coffee?"

"No, thanks."

She had dropped on the table her black-and-white plastic handbag. Now she clicked it open and shook out a pack of Philip Morris. She still didn't look at Henry, but round the room; at the rows of model aeroplanes, at the tanks, at the paperback editions. "Becoming quite a night bird, aren't you?"

"I don't know about that," Henry said.

"Did you enjoy the party?"

"What party?"

"Last night. Santiago's."

"Oh. That. Yes."

"Not really your scene, was it?" He was still standing by the door, seemingly not fully awake; so she lit her own cigarette, fumbling the Flaminaire from her handbag and holding it in her hand after she had finished. "I'm beginning to wonder if it's really mine, either."

"Oh," Henry said. He moved away from the door, leaving it ajar, and went to sit, cautiously, on the end of his bed. He watched her toss the lighter a few inches into the air and catch it; one, two, three times. "...Henry."

"Yes?"

"What do you think I ought to do?"

"About...?"

"About Santiago."

She'd been drinking again, Henry thought. Or maybe not. It was hard to be sure. But her eyes didn't appear to be focussing properly. "...Well," she said, "and all that crowd. They're such *aimless* sort of people."

"They're on holiday, aren't they? I don't suppose they're like that when they're working."

"But do they work? Photographers? Film actresses? And ... Oh, I suppose they do. In a way. But not like us."

"Santi works."

"But not like you and me."

"Still, he isn't *aimless*, exactly."

"I suppose we earn money. It's not the same thing. But these people ... I don't know. I just don't know what I ought to do."

She uncrossed her legs and stood up. On the near shelf there was a model of a Bloodhound earth-to-air missile, complete with trailer; she stooped to examine it, the cigarette stuck unattractively in the corner of her mouth. "You made your decision from the start, didn't you? You keep yourself to yourself. I admire that."

"I don't think I follow you," Henry said.

"Well, you've got your little hobbies, haven't you?—and you don't care very much about all the rest of it. Getting on with people ... That kind of thing. And maybe that isn't quite as silly as I used to think." The model had a tiny handle; turning it, you erected the missile to a firing

67

position. She turned it. "Does it fire?"

"What?"

"Can you shoot it off?" She turned to face him and mimed one-handed, *wheeeee-eeee*. "No," Henry said. "I'm afraid not." And she turned back again.

"Ah, well. As the Americans say, that figures. It's what I like about this room of yours. Nothing in it's for real. They're all models."

Henry shrugged. He was sure now that she'd been drinking. He couldn't for the life of him make out what it was that she wanted.

"... But at least you can *see* they're models. These people, Santi's set ... They fool you. You think they're real. Human beings. And all the time ... I mean, it's *all* like that in Torrevedra. I'm not sure of anything any more."

"Why are you telling me all this?" Henry said, none too graciously. She took no notice, though. He might not have spoken.

"Just one thing I *do* know—my parents'd have kittens, if I did. My father more than my mother, oddly enough. If they ever found out. Of course there's no reason why they should ... but *if* they did. I suppose, up to now, that's the one thing that's stopped me. Silly, isn't it? Just dreary old middle-class mor ... Silly. But there it is."

She had moved a couple of feet to the left now and was poking idly at something else. "Stopped you from what?" Henry asked. "And look, be careful, will you?"

"I *told* you. From Santiago."

"You mean ... going to bed ... ?"

"Well, of course. And I wouldn't mind. And if I don't, he'll get me the sack."

"Oh, he wouldn't do that. I shouldn't think so."

"He would too. I can see his point of view. What the hell am I doing with a job like this, if ...In a *place* like this ... Oh, I can see his point of view all right. But some-

how I just can't get round to ... Well, what's wrong with
me, then? What's wrong with *us*?"

"Why us?" Henry said coldly. She was getting to be
practically incoherent. And anyway, he was tired.

"Because we're the same, really. Everyone thinks you're
square as all get-out, and so you are, but then you don't
pretend to be anything else. Me—I *am* pretending. But for
some stupid reason I can't admit it."

"You could get another job. Supposing you did get the
sack—what would it matter?"

"Just exactly what my parents'd say." She pirouetted,
not gracefully, on one heel and stalked back to the chair.
"I'm just filling in time—that's what they think. Pretty
soon I'll be getting married to some bloody landowner
from Cordoba or wherever or some businessman or even
some bloody lawyer—you know, just like all the others—
only it's the done thing now to get a job to fill in time, just
like it was the done sodding thing for Mama to sit on a
bench for six days a week inside a convent and sally out on
Sundays in a mantilla. So if I *don't* get to start sleeping
around, the alternative's even awfuller. I mean, a bloody
middle-class Spanish marriage—you couldn't wish *that* on
me, could you? The ultimate in boredom, God, we've had
that, we've *had* all that creaky set-up, it's even phonier than
the set-up here. There have to be ... I don't know ... real
people somewhere. But not here. And not there either. It's
like I said. I'm not sure of anything, not any more."

It was odd, in a way, that this steamingly emotional
indictment of Spanish society should come from Anita—
of all people. Martin and Cipriano and Ramona didn't
seem ever to indulge in rhetoric. Henry's sense of the
ironical wasn't well developed, but even he could see that
it was all very odd. Anita was rich—damn it. "You've got
money, haven't you? You're free to do anything you
damned well like. I just don't see why all this song and
dance."

She sat down in the chair again and stubbed out the cigarette, half-smoked, in the blue metal ashtray with TORREVEDRA S.A. printed round the rim. Henry couldn't see her face because she had leaned forwards and her hair had fallen across it, but he knew, without knowing how he knew, that she had started to cry. She was crying quite silently; her shoulders didn't shake, her shoulders didn't move, but she was certainly crying. Henry knew it in the same way that he knew she had been drinking; and just as he had felt vaguely irritated before, now he felt vaguely uncomfortable. She had problems—well, all right, but what made them his business? And above all, right now?

—when he had other things to think about?

"Look," he said. "The thing is, it's a bit late."

"Yes. I'll go."

"I'm sorry if ... I'm probably a bit tired. Can't we talk about all this some other time?"

"I don't suppose there'll be any need." She picked up her handbag and got up, looking straight towards him now and this time as though really seeing him. No tears; just large brown eyes shining in the dim light. That was the way she cried. Without tears. "I just felt like talking tonight. And anyway, you're right. What you said."

"I didn't say anything."

"You did, in a way. No one else wants to know, is what you said. And yes—you're right."

She walked towards the door. "Would you come out with me?" Henry said, and the question stopped her dead.

"Go ... *out* with you?"

"Yes. Sssss ... Sunday evening, maybe. We can ... can ... can ..." He hadn't stuttered in years. It was most peculiar. "Can *talk* about it."

"And maybe hold hands at the pictures?"

"All right. Sorry. Forget it."

"I'd like that."

"You would?"

"Yes. Well, don't look so aback-taken, it's not very flattering."

"I didn't think you would. That's all. I mean ... *like* it."

"Serves you right," Anita said. "This is the first time I've ever known you to act on an impulse." He opened the door for her and watched her sudden, unexpected smile; she was pretty when she smiled, there was no denying it. "And at least you listened to me. Thank you for listening."

"That's all right," Henry said.

Ramona used a plastic funnel to fill three two-pint thermos flasks. There was none left over, which was just as well. Seven years back, in a village not very far from Madrid whose name no one wishes to remember, an amateur chemist had found himself with several tablespoonfuls more jelly than his immediate requirements had indicated, and had tried to get rid of the stuff by pouring it down his kitchen sink. No one is now able to remember *his* name, either; it is not commemorated in the local cemetery, since his body was never buried there. Burial was hardly, in the circumstances, a practical proposition.

She poured the jelly into thermos flasks because jelly is also sensitive to temperature. This was something else which in Spain—where the temperature inside a closed car can actually reach three centigrade figures—some people had learnt the hard way. But not Ramona. Ramona was careful. She stoppered the flasks and put them, one by one, in the blue plastic storage bag, lined with foam rubber. Then she put the storage bag in the steel ice-box, which closed with a padlock. Then she put the ice-box into the big refrigerator. This, while Henry peeled off his rubber gloves and rinsed his hands under the faucet. He was glad it was all over. One of the reasons why it is so easy to make mistakes is because the fumes of the acid give you a splitting headache; Henry had worn a gauze surgical mask but even so, he had a headache now. A bad one.

"There's coffee in the kitchen," Ramona said.

"Good."

"Make some, while I finish clearing up in here. I shall be four or five minutes."

"I'll help you."

"No."

There was a glass percolator on the stove and the coffee inside smelt most appetising. Henry poured himself out a large cup and added—cautiously, meticulously; in his mind he still crouched over the work-bench—two level teaspoonfuls of sugar. Stirred, peering down into the cup as he did so, watching the swirl of dark bubbles at the rim, the curl of the vortex forming around the slim metal shaft of the spoon; inhaled, the smell rising to his nostrils as millions of molecules leapt, broke and were dispersed into the soft, warm air.

It's not dangerous, making jelly, if you're careful. But you're glad when it's all over. You have a nasty headache, but in spite of it all the senses seem sharpened; your impressions rush in a skelter towards a brain that seems too muzzy to receive them, yet can't reject them outright. The effect is hallucinatory, in a way. Henry pulled back a chair and sat at the kitchen window, resting his elbow on the crosspiece of the iron lattice; the air was no cooler there than inside the kitchen, but in the street there was moonlight and the moonlight rested his eyes. In the house next door, a radio was playing loudly and—like the night before—playing flamenco; a harsh woman's voice agonising against a death-rattle of handclaps. But the stridency and even the loudness seemed to be softened or absorbed by the moonlight and by the dark cobbles of the street, to be given—though it was near—a quality of remoteness. This though, or perhaps because, all else was silent; completely silent. The shadows of the houses, of palm trees, all were motionless.

I know what we'll do, Henry thought. I'll take her to San Andres.

(The idea coming to him suddenly, as out of nowhere.)

Then Ramona opened the door and padded on her plimsolled feet across the stone floor to the stove. She, too, poured herself out a cup of coffee and came to sit opposite him, holding the cup (it had no saucer) in both her hands with her elbows tucked in against her waist. Then she, too, craned her neck to savour the aroma before sipping; the cords that ran from the line of her jawbone to the base of her throat stood out prominently. The skin there was very pale, and there were deep creases under her chin. She certainly wasn't young. But *how* old...? Henry wondered. Thirty? Forty? He couldn't guess. There are girls of twenty at San Andres who you'd think were sixty; haggard, toothless, skeletal. Ramona was none of those things. The pallor of her skin held olive shadows. But no, he didn't think that she was young.

"Does your head ache?"

Lowering the cup, she nodded. There was that quality of repose that never left her; that wasn't a young woman's quality, and maybe it made her seem older than she really was. But perhaps it wasn't a woman's quality at all. Women weren't, in Henry's experience, restful.

"It'll clear up, if we rest for half an hour. That's if you don't have to...?"

"No," Henry said.

There was no hurry. And it was pleasant, sitting in this kitchen. Looking at the moonlight, the shadows.

The radio stopped abruptly. For a few seconds there was silence; complete silence. Then music again, this time a string orchestra. Another station. Henry imagined an old, gnarled hand with dark fingers, patiently twiddling the

73

knob. Adjusting. Correcting. An old, gnarled woman, next door.

"Ramona?"

"Yes."

He noticed that she didn't say, "Yes?" She said, "Yes."

"What we're doing," Henry said. "Do you ever have any difficulty ... thinking of it as being real?"

"It's real. It'll work. *No cabe duda.*"

"I didn't mean making the jelly. *That*'s real all right. I meant, *us* making it. Now. This evening. A little back street at one end of Malaga, and two people getting ready to kill other people. Planning how to do it. And outside, there's nothing. Just moonlight, and some shadows, and a radio playing. You see what I mean?"

He wasn't sure, now that he'd said it, whether he himself did, but,

"Yes," she said. "I see now what you mean."

"It's strange."

"Yes. But then all the things that people do when they are alone are very strange."

"You think so?"

"Of course. That music you hear ... It comes from the house next door. There's a fat woman lives there called Dorita. Every night, after dinner, she sits in the front room with the radio turned on and she plays parcheesi. By herself. Look in through the window and you'll see her. If you speak to her, she'll take no notice. She won't hear you. She isn't there. She's playing parcheesi, all by herself. What could be stranger than that?"

"An old woman?"

"No. She's not very old. But farther up the street there's a *very* old woman. Very old and very ugly. Right now she's lying in bed upstairs, thinking. She is thinking of how to kill her daughter-in-law. She rarely thinks of anything else. She has no particular reason, you understand. But all the same, one day she will do it. Or else she will die herself, because she is very old and suffers from a kidney disease. It's sad. And, yes, it's very strange."

"You think she'll *do* it? But how?"

"She bought from me the other day a large tin of rat poison. I told Margarita, *naturalmente*. And no doubt they'll have got it away from her by now. Oh, they know all about it, of course, and they keep an eye on her. It's strange, but it's not all that unusual. Practically everybody plans to kill somebody else, at some time or other; it's only unusual when you think about it *all the time*. I don't do that. Do you?"

"No," Henry said. "God, no. I don't see how you can."

"It's possible when you're old. When you've nothing else to do. Yes, it's possible."

She got up, as though aware that she had left no room for further argument, and fetched the percolator; stooped to re-fill Henry's cup and then her own. Although he had been working with her, waching her movements, for the past two hours, he was surprised yet again by the combined grace and economy of her gestures; it wasn't *Spanish*, this curious abstinence from all unnecessary effort. She had taken off her white lab jacket and now wore an old and very thin green cotton sweater; there were dark stains under its armpits, and under it the movement of her breasts and— as he now realised—the outline of her nipples was perfectly evident. Yet he wasn't embarrassed. She was comfortable that way. So was he.

"I suppose," she said, having during this interval thought on the topic a little more deeply, "it's unusual to plan to kill people you've never met. The other, I would say, is natural. But perhaps what you and I are doing... Yes. Maybe you're right. Maybe it *is* unusual."

"I think that's what I meant," Henry said. "It was just that I couldn't put my finger on it." *No podía echarme el dedo encima* was what he said; and he saw her smile. It was a quiet, unobtrusive smile; feminine because complacent,

complacent for no apparent reason. "... Isn't that right?"

"I understand you, Henry. Perfectly."

"But you wouldn't say that? In Spanish?"

"Don't worry about things like that. You can say things in Spanish that we can't say, and think things that we can't think. That's an advantage. As a foreigner, that's your strength. And we need your strength—Cipriano and I. Don't try to become a Spaniard, Henry. Don't try to change."

"Have you worked with foreigners before?"

"There was an Italian, once. But the Italians are very like us. The English are different."

"I'm half Spanish," Henry said. "My mother was Spanish."

"I don't care. You're an Englishman, *chiquito*." But she broke off to laugh. "I know. I'm too dogmatic. You're right to pick me up. I am not the Pope." Laughing again; Henry could see the spittle gleaming on her regular but slightly over-large front teeth. "And even if I were, it's good to laugh at oneself—once in a while. Even when there's little else to laugh at, there is always oneself. Me, being serious." And she pulled her lips downwards, parodying despondency. "*Muy seria, muy digna.* No, it's not good to be serious. Not all the time."

Far away down the street, dogs were barking; a faint, anaesthetised yapping. The night was becoming immense.

"Cipriano's serious," Henry said. "A thinking man, he calls himself."

"Cipriano is dependable."

"Tomorrow morning..."

He left the phrase unended, without knowing why. It was late; his head was clearing; but he still felt reluctant to get up and leave, to lose himself in the vastness of that waiting night. Then from the next room there came the sharp, reptilian rattle of the telephone bell; it was uncannily as though he had anticipated that sound, had broken off short accordingly. Ramona put her cup down on the floor beside the chair and went to answer the call. It wasn't a long one. She came back almost at once.

"Well," she said. "Now we know."

"Know what?"

"Today is Saturday. And Hernandez leaves Madrid next Tuesday morning.'

"For Malaga?"

"Yes." She ran the tip of her tongue across her lips; blinked down at him sleepily, like a cat. "He's to meet Martorell at half past eight. Next Tuesday evening."

"That gives us just three days," Henry said.

"Yes. So there it is. Now we know."

The track came to an end at a refuse dump. Once a week, the dustcarts from the neighbouring villages tipped their loads there; once a year, a gang from the Department of Sanitation at Fuengirola came along, raked the rubbish into a great twelve-foot-high pile and then burnt it. They wore regulation gas-masks, because the refuse was putrid and ponged to heaven. They usually did this in September. From the end of May onwards, not many people visited that vicinity, except for those who handled the dustcarts; and even they approached with an increasing reluctance. It wasn't difficult to avoid the place, after all. You knew when you were getting near.

"A nice quiet place," Cipriano said.

"Di-gog," Henry answered. He had a handkerchief over his nose and mouth.

They parked the Citroën to the left of the track, in the shade of the cluster of locust trees. The two canvas packs were on the back seat. Cipriano slung one over his shoulder; Henry preferred to carry the other tucked under his arm. Canvas straps have been known to break. He stood waiting while Cipriano wound up the windows and locked the car. Beyond the locust trees there was a narrow, dusty valley, with rocks to either side. At the head of the valley there was a derelict stone building, roofless, its walls crumbling, and a little nearer, a dilapidated wooden shed.

"Is that it?"

"That's it," Cipriano said, looking at his watch.

"What's it supposed to be?"

"They tried to build a road through there a couple of years ago. God knows why. And then they had to give it up, for the usual reasons. Ran out of money, couldn't get through that outcrop, the boss went on holiday—anything you like. That was the foreman's hut. For storing tools, equipment—the usual thing. The cable's still there, is the point. I checked."

"It's quiet all right," Henry said. Beyond the valley there were rocks, rocks and more rocks, ash-grey and brown. Far to the south and beyond a steep dip in the hills, the flattened sea. The heat was building up already. "You think anyone will hear?—when it goes off?"

"Maybe. There's a farmhouse a couple of kilometres away, behind that crest. But no one'll be bothered." Cipriano's eyes were creased into pouchy slits by the bright sunlight. "They were blasting on that road, of course. No other way to get through the rock. They'll reckon a stick of explosive got left behind and went off by itself. I doubt if anyone'll even want to take a look."

"Not with this smell, they won't."

"It's not so bad, down there."

"Let's go, then."

They set off together down the slope. The shrill chirping of the cicadas was stilled as they moved through the trees, started up again as soon as they had gone past. Once they were clear of the trees altogether, the beeping rose to a high-pitched haze of sound behind them, diminishing gradually as they descended. Such breeze as there was blew gently up the valley, and once past the lip the smell ceased to be noticeable; but the rocks trapped and reflected the sun and it was certainly no cooler. From a closer range, the relics of the road were clear enough; the surface of the bed of the valley was scarred but perfectly even, and the danger of an accidental stumble virtually disappeared. "Where does it go to? The road?"

"Mijas, eventually," Cipriano said. "But it's a good long way."

They reached the hut some five minutes later. The wooden door was splintered and stood ajar, but the hut had no windows. The darkness inside was profound.

"Wait till we get used to it," Cipriano said.

They put their packs down on the hard earth floor and sat down beside them, their backs to the wall. Cipriano lit a cigarette.

Gradually, the darkness receded. Not, however, revealing very much of interest in the process; the hut was almost completely empty. There was a badly-smashed wooden table to their left—packing-case boards supported by three splay legs and a strut on the wall; behind the table there were other packing-cases, all split open and, in some cases, reduced to a mass of powdery splinters. "They've had a look round, you see," Cipriano said. "They've cleaned the place out."

"Who have?"

"Here in Spain, there's always somebody. Any place that gets left abandoned—it's picked clean as a whistle within a week. Tools, nails, planks—any old thing at all. It's amazing, really."

"What about that, then?"

In the far corner, behind the packing-cases, there was a shallow pile of dry straw and a couple of threadbare grey Army blankets. "Yes," Cipriano said. "That's more recent. Somebody's been using the place."

"Tramps?"

"Tramps don't come this way. Lovers, more like it."

"From the village?"

"From the village. From Africa. From the moon. No need to worry."

Crouching, Henry investigated further. On the floor beside the blankets there was a burnt-down candle end; that was all. "It's at night they come here, then. Whoever it is." The far corner of the hut was empty, except for a piece of sacking, mouldered, gone to dust. Henry lifted it a little, and small many-legged creatures scurried for sanctuary.

"I don't see any cable."

"It's here," Cipriano said. "We'll find it."

He finished his cigarette first, though, shredding at last the dog-end to tobacco dust on the sole of his shoe. Then they searched for the cable together. It was Cipriano who found it, naturally enough; it was his job. Someone had torn away the socket and pins, leaving the terminal wires stripped and bare; he took a new terminal from his canvas pack and, squatting down, whistling, rebuilt the connection. "I'd have had to do this anyway. The old one would have rusted away. You'd be surprised how metal deteriorates, round these parts. It's the sea air."

"The sea's five miles away."

"Even so."

Squatting in the near-darkness, screwing, testing and, all the time, whistling very softly. In the end he reached again for his pack and took out the telephone; laid aside the receiver, inverted the cradle and commenced to unscrew the base. "Ready?"

"When you are."

"Come on, then."

He moved on his knees nearer to the door, where the light was better, and held the inverted cradle in both hands, resting his wrists and elbows on the floor. Henry took the thermos flask from its white cotton-waste nest inside his pack and span off its white plastic top; then, more carefully, the interior plug. He knelt, adjusting his position, his balance. "Right?"

"Right."

He poured the jelly, a few spoonfuls at a time, into the telephone's black plastic mouth. When the flask was emptied, he set it down, no less carefully, beside the wall and picked up the black disc with the narrow thread that Cipriano had just unscrewed. "It'd be easier, on a table."

"Get on with it," Cipriano said.

Henry's fingers moved slowly, cautiously, efficiently. The disc, lightly oiled, turned smoothly on its groove.

"... Okay."

"It's tight?"

"Yes."

"Good."

Cipriano turned the cradle very gently in his hands, setting it the right way up. He left it standing on the floor while he replaced the receiver on its stand, plugged in the insulated wire, wiped his hands on his shirt. "How long?"

"Seven minutes," Henry said.

"We could do it quicker. If we had to."

"But not unless we had to."

"Easier on a table. You said so yourself."

Cipriano seemed a little short of breath.

"Pues bien. Estamos."

"Estamos," Henry said. He was putting the flask back in its bag. Cipriano, too, collected his equipment. They looked at the telephone in silence for a few moments, then went outside. Henry stood beside the door, eyes screwed up against the renewed brilliance of the sunlight, and took a deep breath of hot, dry air. There were the rocks again, scattered over the tortured earth. Beyond the hut, a few stunted trees. Then the vacant blue of the sky where, high above the hills, a kestrel drifted. "Look," Cipriano said.

Close to the wooden wall of the hut and just clear of the door, the earth was imprinted with the marks of a tyre or tyres. Not deeply—the soil was too dry and hard—but quite clearly; it was strange they hadn't seen the tracks when they'd arrived. "A motor-bike," Cipriano said. "Leans against the wall. See?"

"It's been here more than once."

"Plenty of times. Tramps don't use motor-bikes."

"No."

They walked up to the scrub of trees where they had left the Citroën parked. The slope was steeper than Henry had supposed, but with the thermos flask now empty, the going seemed oddly easy. He stood by the car while Cipriano unlocked the door and got in.

"What time do you make it?"

"Five to eleven," Henry said.

"Give us the pack."

Henry winced as Cipriano tossed it on to the back seat. A flask that has been, till recently, packed full of jelly deserves respect. "I'll send the balloon up at eleven-fifteen."

"Right," Henry said.

"And I'll give it another jog at eleven-twenty. But the first ring'll do the trick. Here." He handed Henry the field glasses through the open window. "Keep out of sight as far as you can."

"Okay."

Henry walked, while Cipriano was backing the car, into the shade of the locust trees and sat down there. It was a pity, he thought, he hadn't brought anything to drink.

You got very quickly accustomed to the stench. After the first five minutes, you hardly noticed it, or noticed it only when you thought about it. And the sea breeze had mounted slightly; enough to raise an occasional dustdrift from the hillside, especially in one or two places where the hooves of horses, descending to the valley, had loosened the bone-dry earth. He and Cipriano would, of course, have left no recognisable tracks in their rubber-soled shoes; and in any case, no one would be looking for them.

A motor-bike, that was different. That was heavy.

Imagine doing it in a place like that. On a trampled earth floor, sunbaked as hard as brick. Candlelight, and a couple of mouldering blankets. Surely there'd be better places ... ? Nowhere more private, of course. Cipriano had certainly chosen the site for that very reason; its isolation was complete. There was next to no chance of their experiment being disturbed. And privacy ... It all depends on what you value. In Torrevedra, privacy had a low priority. In the villages up the hills, a very high one. Decency and discomfort tended to go together, in Spanish tradition.

But where *was* the Spanish tradition nowadays? Where could you find it? Enshrined down there in a wooden hut, far enough from the rest of humanity for the gasps of youthful lust to go unheeded? Or in the back room of a chemist's shop, where at ten yards' distance a mad fat woman played with dice and counters and where a very sane woman planned an equally meaningless game of double execution? Or could it be in Torrevedra, where a young and very pretty girl talked about not knowing anything any more? Yes, what about Anita? Wooden huts weren't in her line, but then penthouse couches weren't, either. Or at least, she said they weren't. Of course she was stupid. But stupid in an interesting way. He'd have no more idea than he usually did of what to say to her when they went out that night, but probably he wouldn't need to say much. She'd do all the talking.

He'd take her to San Andres and see what she said.

Or was that stench, too, of a kind that you got accustomed to? Surely not. Human beings weren't rubbish to be disposed of. It was at San Andres, after all, that he himself, three years ago, had decided what he had to do. Had decided to talk to Martin in London. To try and help. Before San Andres, you could say that he'd been stupid, too. Aimless. The very word she'd used. It might not affect her in the same way, but then again it might. It was worth trying.

Henry looked at his wrist-watch. Eleven fourteen. He rolled sideways from his seated position until he was lying flat on his stomach, his elbows steadied on the hot flat rock directly in front of him. He raised the field-glasses and focused them—steadily, carefully—on the wooden hut.

The Citroën rounded the corner, pebbles rattling in a cloud of dust. It pulled up and Cipriano wound down the window. "Well, how did she blow?"

"She didn't," Henry said.

"Didn't . . . ?"

"Nothing."

"It must have done."

"Nothing," Henry said. "See for yourself."

Cipriano swung open the door but, instead of getting out, sat back in the seat, one foot still thrust out to hold down the brake unnecessarily. Then he reached over to switch off the ignition. "What went wrong?"

"I don't know. Nothing's happened. That's all."

"*Coño,*" Cipriano said.

He swung himself out of the car and they walked together over to the locust trees. The strap of the field-glasses was too long; they bumped against Henry's waist. In fact, nobody needed field-glasses. The hut was still there, obviously.

"You were right," Cipriano said. "This thing needs ironing out."

"What happens when you ring?"

"Nothing at all. You don't hear the bell ringing, because there's no bloody bell. The detonator's wired to the trembler. A dead phone is what it should sound like."

"And did it?"

"Yes. Both times. I'll have to try again."

"It's damned hot here," Henry complained.

You could imagine them soldiers, crossing the hill and marching into the rifle-barrel sun, a heartbeat's range away; breaking ranks where the grey rocks exploded, crouching breathless on the mountainside. Then the leaves would shimmer in the south breeze, their multiple coating of fine dust reflecting a quartzine glitter, and once again they'd be trees, ilex and Spanish oak, heat-stunted, earth-stained, struggling the length of the narrow valley. The loose soil clinging to their roots would once in a long while slide away, raising a tiny whitish-grey puff, and pebbles would rattle softly as they bounced down the slope, bringing to mind a vague astronomy of machine-guns, a distant ricochet from some unknown and unimaginable war. Perhaps the advance had already begun; the wind and the sun and the silvery dust were maybe marshalled now for their counter-attack; soon the trees would move down towards the sea, invading and overwhelming the derelict villas and waterless lawns, breaking in a great wave over the four-lane highway, leaving the concrete hotels picked clean as skeletons in their path, moving down till at last this hill-dust was mixed with the sand and all would be then as now it was here, motionless and parched under the aching blue of the sky. Torremolinos, gone; San Andres, gone; nothing but this, the desert and the circling eagles. Motionless and silent; the pebbles still would fall and the waves beat on the empty beach, but how can there be sound where no living ear can hear it? All sound leads to silence, wants to be silence, especially the loudest sounds of all; the scream of a crashing car, the whipping blast of explosive. Far down in the valley, the sun was gleaming on something small and shiny. Probably a broken bottle. Henry rubbed at his eyes and thought about beer. It was certainly hot.

The Citroën came round the corner again. This time as soon as it was parked Cipriano got out; stood legs apart and hands on hips staring crossly down across the valley. "So nothing."

"Nothing," Henry said. "And nobody's come this way, either. What I'd call a nice quiet Sunday morning."

"It could be a dud detonator."

"Yes, that happens."

"Or it could be the relay isn't tripping. I've been plugging away at it this last half-hour ... trying to activate it ... but it's no good. This afternoon, I'll try it with the marker. Damn it," Cipriano said. "It mustn't happen Tuesday night. That's the point." He walked away a few paces and kicked at a stone lying in the track; it disappeared over the lip of the verge, rattled vaguely down the scree beneath. "But the bugger was working all right yesterday. I tested the line three times. It *has* to be the detonator."

It was so obvious that he was talking in order to convince himself that Henry didn't bother to reply. There was, in any case, nothing to say. Cipriano went on staring across the valley, at rocks, trees, hills, cloudless sky. The hut was invisible now behind the crest. "It's a flop," Cipriano said. *"Un fracaso total."*

"What's this marker thing?"

"I can check the switching system with it. The trouble is, all it'll do is tell us if there's anything wrong with the relay. And whether there is or isn't, there won't be a hell of a lot that I can do about it."

"We could take a look at the detonator," Henry said.

"Oh, for God's sake. It's coming up to forty degrees in the shade. That jelly'll have turned to water by now. We can't even take the risk of going in there to blow it, let alone take out the detonator. It'll go if you breathe on it."

86

"So we just leave it there?"

"It'll blow of its own accord. Sooner or later. And probably sooner."

"But someone might ... That chap on the motor-bike. What if they go there again?"

"Then that'll solve the problem," Cipriano said.

He opened the car door again and took a packet of cigarettes from the glove shelf; a blue packet. Ideales. "Smoke?"

"No, thanks," Henry said.

He still felt thirsty. His throat was dry.

Saturday nights.

The field-glasses were still slung round his neck. He took them off and got to his feet.

"I'm going down."

"What for?"

"I want to take a look."

"That's stupid," Cipriano said. *"No hay nada que hacer."*

"If it's the detonator," Henry said, "that's my responsibility. Not yours. I ought to take a look."

"We can't have an accident at this stage. Or at any other. It's just not worth the risk."

"I know what I'm doing."

In fact he wasn't sure that he did.

It was hotter than before, down in the valley. The breeze had died. The skin of his face and neck prickled as the sweat, forced through the open pores, was evaporated on the instant by a sun-heat that seemed to press down on him from above, like a tangible weight. With some twenty yards still to go, he stopped and looked at the hut, at the black angled slit of the half-open door. From here on, he'd be in the fragmentation area. Even at that close range, the heat haze from the rocks made the outline of the hut quiver and shake. The valley was a sun-trap. Forty degrees? Down there, it was all of fifty-five. Pushing a hundred and twenty fahrenheit. He looked at his wristwatch. One o'clock. Incredible, the difference that two hours made.

Saliva had formed a sticky ball at the back of his throat. He had to swallow twice to get rid of it and even then, it seemed only to form a knot in his gullet. It wasn't that he was afraid. He was careful, he was always careful with high explosives; if you're careful, you need never be afraid. Treat them with proper respect, and there's nothing to fear. He walked slowly forwards to the door and pushed it, gently, a little further open. The drop in the temperature, when he entered its shade, brought out the sweat in a sudden flooding rush; he took out a handkerchief to wipe his face, his neck, his hands. He wasn't afraid. It was the heat.

All the same, Cipriano was right. When you take an unnecessary risk, you're not being careful. Every precaution means every possible precaution. But then, he thought, I know what I'm doing...

He squatted down, frog-like, just inside the door. The telephone sat—also somehow frog-like, reptilian—on the floor in front of him but out of his reach, four feet away. The cable, the connection, the plug were all in place. Nothing wrong at all. To get at the detonator, you had to pull out the cable plug; then you drew the detonator from its socket with a pair of tweezers. Pulling out the plug was the tricky part. There mustn't be any jerk. In the ordinary way, you'd screw clamps round the cradle. Slowly. Carefully. Henry didn't have clamps. He carried tweezers, a screwdriver, pliers. The sweat was pouring down his face. The handkerchief was still in his hand, and he used it again.

There was a smell, somewhere, that he didn't recognise. Not the rubbish smell, the stench of rotten garbage. Something different. He looked at the telephone. Its black plastic gleamed faintly in the shadows. The dial, smooth and blank, was turned towards him. Nothing happened.

Naturally not. What the hell *could* happen?

He remembered a story he'd once heard of an old Spanish peasant who spent hours at a time in the church, before a painted statue of Christ. When they asked him what he thought about, he said, "I look at Him ... and He looks at me." It was like that now. He was really thinking of absolutely nothing. He was looking at the telephone, and the telephone was looking at him. How long a time had he already been there, squatting, staring...? The question was as meaningless as the other. Three minutes, five, ten. They looked at each other, and nothing happened. Nothing and everything.

On his hands and knees, he crawled up to it.

The jelly would have turned to liquid in this great heat; have turned, in effect, to nitro-glycerine. It could blow for any reason or for no reason at all. You treat all explosives with respect; but for nitro-glycerine, respect isn't enough. You treat it with awe. Nitro-glycerine is power unleashed through caprice; nitro-glycerine is Old Testament godhead. Unthinking destruction. Henry bowed over it, peering down. Fragmentation statistics are for theologians. This was the real thing, the Immanent Presence that, if it so willed, could smash him into tiny fragments of quivering flesh, of splintered bone, of blood, could smear him over a blast-flattened circle of forty yards' diameter. Oh God, Henry thought. Not this time.

Spare me.

...and knew, with startling suddenness, that he *was* afraid. Fear churned in his stomach; he was sick with fear, fear of a kind outside all his experience; he was hypnotised by terror of the telephone. He couldn't move. Every muscle in his body had gone rigid. Only his mouth moved, jerked; his lips were pulled farther and farther back in an agonising rictus. He felt no pain; this was different to pain; you wait for pain to pass. This would never pass. Time had stopped. This was eternity.

But the corded sinews of his throat, too, were contracting, and the air forcing itself slowly out of his paralysed lungs made a harsh, vibrant sound against his pharynx; a growl, a croak. It was the sound that saved him. He put out a hand and, with the tip of one finger, touched the telephone. The surface was smooth and hard and already filmed with the finest imaginable of dusts. His face was now calm, relaxed, an emotional blank. He rocked his weight back on to his heels and stood up, then turned to walk slowly out of the hut. The waiting heat came at him fiercely, like a burning wave; he marched through it steadily, heading up the slope, going back to Cipriano, and the car, and to some other destiny.

3

The evening turned out to be another *fracaso*. Again, he couldn't see quite where the trouble was. Detonator, trip-switch, cable ... anything at all. Anita wasn't like Ramona. Anita was careless, Anita was difficult. And he, Henry, wasn't good with people. He knew it.

"Why in God's name have we come here?"

"It's interesting," Henry said.

"Interesting?"

"Extraordinary, I mean."

"It's just horrible and dirty. That's all."

A sudden runnel of foul-smelling liquid coursed past their feet. No visible source, no apparent destination; just motiveless energy, liquid, brown, glistening. "When you think about Torrevedra," Henry said, "it's only eight miles away or so. You take a 'bus, you walk a hundred yards, and you're in ... this."

"I suppose you think this is the *real* Spain. A sort of bloody tourist attraction. I suppose you think I haven't seen places like this before. Oh, come on. Let's get out of here."

"All right," Henry said. And they went on walking, side by side, down the street; except that you couldn't call it a street. Black gritty sand, hard and furrowed like corrugated iron. And to either side, the shacks; wood, rough undressed stone, and palm-leaf roofs. Naked and sunblackened children crawled here and there on the grit and through the rubble, pawing at this, snouting at that; older, wizened, woman-like creatures sat on wicker chairs in the near-darkness of the windowless huts. There were no men in San Andres; there was no work in San Andres. The woman-creatures brought up children on fifteen pounds a year. In

San Andres, they didn't even beg; they'd lost the initiative. Only in a near-perfect climate is the nadir of human existence made possible; elsewhere, they'd have died. Here they stayed alive—if you called it living. They didn't leave. There was nowhere else to go.

"I thought," Henry said, "it might be a kind of reminder. That's all."

"A reminder?"

"To put things in perspective. That's what it does for me. This isn't the real Spain, but it *is* the real problem. All the rest—"

"Problem who to?"

"To the people who live here. Of course."

"These people don't have problems. Pigs don't have problems. They don't *have* to live here, do they? They choose to. This is the way they like it."

"But how could anyone *like* it?"

"Well, exactly. No normal person would. They're not human beings, that's why. They're animals. You can't do a thing for them—everybody knows that. I mean, it's been tried."

No, Henry thought; San Andres hadn't been a good idea. Because basically Anita was right. People have problems because that's the way they like it, that's how they know they're alive. Anita, she herself had problems; she wanted to talk about them, but she didn't want them solved. Not really. And she certainly couldn't be bothered with other people's. They weren't interesting. This place wasn't interesting. There was only one thing that interested Anita and that was herself; herself she found truly fascinating. The old Spanish egotism, no doubt; but any way you looked at it, she was a little bitch. So it hadn't been a good idea at all.

Never mind. They'd pick up the 'bus again and go on to the Club de Golf, the swimming pool, the American Bar. Or they could walk there along the beach. It was only a couple of kilometres. Anita liked walking, or she'd said she did. "This is where it all started for me," Henry said. "But I suppose it wouldn't affect you in the same way. There's no reason why it should."

"Where what all started?"

Yes. What, exactly? He knew what he meant. But he didn't know how to explain. It was always the same. Walking, side by side. He could never get through. *No hay nada que hacer*. Maybe, taking a risk again ... but how? He couldn't see how.

Anita wasn't like Ramona. Careless, difficult, yes; but there was more to it than that. She was younger. But no. That wasn't it, either. Quite suddenly,

"I've never been with a girl," Henry said.

"You mean, alone with one? Like now?"

"No. *Been* with one."

"Oh," Anita said, and nodded.

"I'm like you, in a way. I'm grown up and all that, but I've still never been with a girl. It's bloody silly."

"But what's that got to do with anything?"

Yes. What, exactly?

He didn't know why he'd said that. Unless, at that moment, he'd really been speaking to Ramona. With Ramona, it could have passed for a simple statement of fact. But he knew that he hadn't been speaking to Ramona. He'd spoken to Anita, out of some kind of desperation; a confession, an open admission, a charge to blow the lines of communication open at last. Without fully realising it, he'd pressed the detonator button and *phut*. It hadn't gone off. She'd nodded, in total incomprehension. He couldn't blame her. He couldn't understand it himself.

"I don't understand girls. Other people. It has to do with everything, in a way."

"But why should that help?"

"Why should what help?"

"That. What you said. Supposing you ... had it off with

someone, why would that help? I'd have thought there'd be nothing easier. For a man."

"Oh yes. I know there are places you can go to. I said it was silly."

Flies rose from a mangled something at Henry's feet and hovered noisily in the air for a few seconds, several clinging with small moist suckers to his face and neck until he brushed them away. They were on the outskirts of the shanty village now, the black sands stretching away unbroken to the east.

"I'd have thought that at Torrevedra there'd be ... I mean, there's nothing wrong, is there? With you?"

"Physically?"

"Or anything like that?"

"No. I don't think so. Nothing."

"Why did you say, *like me*?"

"Did I?"

"Back there. You said, *I'm like you*. And then that you'd never—"

"Well, what you were saying the other night. Isn't that what you were on about?"

"Oh God, no. You misunderstood me. I'd do it like a shot, it's not that I'm *worried* about it—"

"You would do it, yes, but have you?"

"It's not—"

"Well, *have* you?"

"No," Anita said.

"There you are, then."

"But if I wanted to, if I really wanted to..."

"Then it has to be that you don't want to."

"It's not that, either."

"Well, but—"

"Oh, I don't *know*, shut *up*, why don't you?" Suddenly, she was furious. Her small brown fists were clenched. "Let's not talk about it. I'm sorry I ever mentioned it. It was probably all a mistake, anyway."

"I thought you wanted to talk about it."

"Well, I don't."

Now they were on the beach. You could call it a beach in as much as you could call the gritty channel between the San Andres shacks a street: the sea was there, certainly, white-topped waves were tumbling and there was a semblance of colour, but the sand was still dark crystalline grit that crunched under their shoes and everywhere was litter, refuse, debris of every describable and indescribable kind. Walking at the edge of the sea and with the onshore breeze blowing, you didn't notice the smell so much, but it was there all the time, there behind them, the smell of San Andres; one great, seething, pullulating rubbish dump.

Anita was right. Out there on the mountains the tin cans, the plastic bags and the discarded newspapers had no significance, were no more than a tiny stain on the great immensity of ash-coloured rock; here on the beach they *had* significance, grew indeed to constitute the whole of reality. They were horrible. The hill villages were poor and were very dirty; but the poverty and the dirt were natural, indigenous. San Andres was something else. San Andres was the bowel-opening of a civilised world, a world of material comfort and convenience—petrol cans and broken bottles, shattered light bulbs and coils of rusted wire, greasy metal struts and broken-down car batteries. What you found up in the hills was good, honest, human shit. This was something else. Filth. No. There wasn't a word for it. Anita was right, but as always she'd missed the point.

"I feel like a bathe," she said, "after this. Or a shower, more like it."

A shower was no good, though. It had to be the wind, the cleansing wind. The grey smoke-plume drifting, and that other, that acrid, bitter scent. For a moment he sensed it in his nostrils, the tang of high explosive, and felt his stomach muscles tighten in response. It was up there in the hills now, waiting; the narrow detonating rod sheathed in

95

its vagina of gelignite; and Cipriano would be up there waiting, too, among the trees, testing out his marker, waiting for the sudden splintering fury of its orgasm. Or perhaps he wasn't waiting. Perhaps he had gone home. Walking, walking. Their footsteps *crunch, crunch*, on the dry black sand. Walking, side by side.

By now he would have given up, would have gone home. Henry should have been there, instead; Henry should have been waiting there, crouched in the shadow of the trees. Better to be there, after all, than to be walking thus, aimlessly, across this slow eternity of grit. Aimless, was what she'd said. And now she'd brought him in, made him one of them; he too was treading the seventh circle to the sound of electric guitars, was walking in the hot black winds. Better to be there, in the hills. He'd have waited there hour after hour; he'd done it before; he was patient. Till nightfall he'd have waited. He wouldn't have been bored. He'd have had his thoughts.

Nightfall. There were still three, four hours to go. At nightfall, perhaps, they'd arrive. Pop pop pop, far off in the distance but drawing nearer. Tonight, Sunday night, or any night; any warm, airless, Mediterranean night; starshine there'd be, the moon in the locust trees, then the scything sweep of the approaching headlamp. Voices...? No. They wouldn't talk. There'd be the warmth of their linked bodies on saddle and pillion, arm circling waist; a gentle, an anticipatory pressure.

... Unzipping her skirt, stepping out of it with that oddly gawky grace, like a colt's. Today, it was the blue one-piece swimsuit. She stooped to spread the towel out on the sand, turned to stretch herself out on it; her eyelids were lowered against the angled sun. The red beach bag was open at her side. Henry sat down heavily beside her. "Don't you have any family, Henry?" He looked at her in some surprise; after so long a silence, he hadn't expected so sudden a question.

"No. My parents are dead."

"No brothers or sisters?"

"No."

"It doesn't help. I wouldn't want to be like them. I mean, like mine."

Henry, too, closed his eyes and lay back. He had no towel beneath him, and the warmth of the sand clutched him instantly, imprisoned him. They had walked perhaps a mile, had left San Andres behind. Here the sand was brown and grey, interspersed with tufts of dry grass and with layers of pebbles. Here there was no one. Only the sun and the lapping sea, and a few fishing boats drifting south. Not even that, when you closed your eyes. Then there was nothing but a glowing red veil, at once transparent and opaque. That, and the close, searching warmth of the sand.

"Your mother was Spanish, wasn't she?"

"Yes," Henry said.

"Where from?"

"She always talked about going back to Alicante. I suppose she was born there."

"You didn't get on with her, then?"

"I had a bad effect on her. She was a bit ... neurotic."

Anita sighed. "*My* parents are all right, really. It's just that they want things to go on ... I don't know. Like back in the eighteenth century or something."

"No one who's rich wants anything to change."

"Everything for you is a matter of being rich. Or poor. And anyway, they're not. Just middle-class-rich. Well off, then."

"Santiago's rich."

"His father is," Anita said. "That's not quite the same thing, either. Santi has his little troubles."

"Does he tell you about them?"

"Sometimes."

Sun worship. Well, why not? The sun is silent. That's

all you ask of a god, nowadays. It's there; you can feel its heat, its strength, on your body. But it never speaks. There's nothing to confuse the relationship; no words, no language. Like sex, it's of the body. The sun's body and yours.

"Why do you think he wants you?"

"Thank you," Anita said. "Thanks very much."

"No, don't be silly. Of course you're pretty, anyone can see that. But for someone like Santiago, there have to be plenty of others. Who ... You know."

"Who're more expeienced."

"Who wouldn't make such a song and dance of it, I was going to say."

"You're the one who's being silly, Henry."

"I don't see how."

"You always think there has to be a reason for everything. Of course there are others. What do you suppose he's doing this evening, while I'm out with you ... ? He's not in love with me. I mean, *love*, you're just like my parents in a way. What's it mean, *love*? He just fancies me. That's all."

"And you?"

A brief silence. In the end she said, briefly as before, "... No."

That probably meant *yes*, Henry decided. He'd read about that, somewhere. Anyway, if it didn't mean *yes*, then the whole thing was bloody ridiculous, which perhaps was the case. Any way you looked at it, girls were stupid.

Ramona wasn't happy about the day's work.

"I have a bad feeling about this one," she said.

"*Tonterías*. Don't come the old gitana on me."

"Gitana, nothing. Other people have feelings, apart from gipsies. You've had them yourself."

Cipriano shook his head. "Not because something didn't work."

"That's just a part of it."

"I've taken the marker to it," Cipriano said patiently. "We know exactly where it's going wrong. It's the selector system. The brushes. The impulses aren't being coded properly. It's ringing on a dead number."

"It's what I said from the beginning. We can't trust the Telefónica. You work for them, you know just how bad the system is."

"It's not the system. It's the bloody equipment. Like everything else in this country." Cipriano was doodling in the ashtray with one end of a match. "I still think it's better than any kind of time-mechanism. But then, the decision's yours."

"What does Henry think?"

"I don't know. I haven't asked."

Sunday evening; and Ramona was smartly turned out for once. Blue cotton skirt, white frilly blouse, and a well-cut bra beneath it; men turned their heads to look at her as they walked past the bar. Cipriano was pleased with her, even though she seemed to be in a difficult mood.

"I have this feeling," she said. "One gets them sometimes."

"Superstition. Others, yes. But not you."

"What about *you*? You're confident?"

He looked at the burnt end of the match, dropped it into the ashtray.

"The boy makes me nervous. I'll admit that."

"Why?"

"*Es un chico muy raro*. He's not one of us."

"Of *us*, in the way you mean, there aren't many left. There have to be new people. Young people. And he knows about explosives. I've seen him work."

"He's odd."

"People who work with explosives often are."

"That's true. Yes, by God, that's true. Remember el

99

Medio Muerto? Now *he* was a weirdo. Liquid oxygen, he used to swear by—they should have had him in the space race, if you ask me. And to look at him, you'd think he *drank* the stuff. Yes, he was a real nutter, no doubt about it."

"Sixty-six, wasn't it? In Bilbao."

"In Bilbao. I never got to hear what happened."

"They machine-gunned the car," Ramona said.

"Yes. Somebody talked, I suppose."

"Somebody talked."

"That was a long time ago," Cipriano said. "And now it's Henry." He hunched up his shoulders in his thin grey jacket. "Damn me if it isn't hotter here, even, than it is in Torrevedra."

"Malaga's a hot town," Ramona said.

A hot town and a noisy town. The bar where they sat was full of people, all talking at the tops of their voices. They themselves made no effort to keep their voices down. There wasn't the remotest chance of their being overheard; they could only just hear each other. The bar was some little way from Larios, from the central district, and had no air conditioning; electric fans in each corner roared unheard against the shouted clatter of conflicting voices, and seemed to cool the room hardly at all.

"Has he got a girl down here?"

"Henry?" Cipriano moved his shoulders again, this time in a shrug. "Not here or anywhere, is my impression."

"Yes. It's a pity."

"I don't know why you say that. Girls are dangerous. Things are difficult enough without that."

"He's young, though," Ramona said. "The young one's don't relax. Henry doesn't seem to. Ever. It would be better—much better—if he did."

"Relaxing is something you have to learn."

"And it's time that *he* learnt."

"Oh, yes," Cipriano said.

"Well? Why not?"

"It wouldn't be the first time you've ... helped out, would it?"

"Helping out is what I'm here for. There's nothing else I *can* do."

"Then what about me?"

"Oh, you, you know how to relax. You said so yourself. You don't have any problems. Besides ... for you and me, there's always afterwards."

"Yes. *Always* afterwards. That's what I complain about."

"It's no good complaining," Ramona said. "We won't be seeing each other again until then. Until this one's over."

"For any special reason?"

"If anything's wrong and they get on to me, Henry has a chance. You don't. It's common sense."

"It's because of the feeling."

"All right," Ramona said. "It's because of the feeling."

To be able to relax, that's very important.

A whiteness in the candlelight. A convolution of limbs. Whiteness and shadows. Then the headlamps, (slow scything sweep), the roar of the motor, and in that cold clarity of light the girl on the blankets, naked, twisted, her white teeth snapping as she bit at the empty air; click, click. Her black hair loose and tumbled. And he in his white jacket watching, watching by the wall. Henry Allanbee, M.D. Diagnosis: hysteria. A bit neurotic. He leaned forwards and struck with his fist at the upturned face, struck again and again. The noise of the motor was growing louder and louder, the light brighter; at any moment now he would hear the whine of the brakes, the scream of the tyres on London asphalt. The girl moaned, twisting, as his hands closed round her throat. His own teeth were loose in his gums, were falling out; his mouth was full of blood and saliva. Louder and harder. Why didn't she scream? Now.

101

Now it would happen. The accident.

Instead, the sudden cacophonous jangle of the telephone bell. It stood there, beside the bed, on the shelf with the model tanks and soldiers; shiny black plastic and white dial, melting as he stared at it, dissolving inwards, then unfurling pointed petals like a great black chrysanthemum; the blast rocking the room, a black wind whistling, a bitter-smelling black flower reaching out for him, engulfing him, while the shrill yelling of the bell went on and on. It swallowed him, the noise and the blackness, and he died ... and, at the same moment, woke up, rolling over on the narrow mattress to switch off the alarm clock. He gazed for a few moments at the empty dial, then let his head fall heavily back on the pillow.

A bad one. He knew it had been a bad one, but that was all he knew. No remembrance. Only of that empty dial; the dial had been in his dream, somehow. He looked again at the clock, and its face was empty no longer. The dial was just as usual. Hands, numbers. Seven fifteen, on a Monday morning.

He hadn't slept well.

Only while he was shaving did he remember the bomb.

He learnt, when he got to the office, that the van Koons had troubles, too. The van Koons had a villa on the upper slopes, somewhere beyond Petrie's place; an elderly, bad-tempered couple. They'd been away for the weekend and the villa had been broken into. Not thieves; just the usual bunch of yobs. Broken glass, smashed furniture, and unspecified depredations in the main bedroom. "They never tell us when they leave the place empty," Gomez said, "and then they kick up the hell of a shindy when something like this happens. *Están como las chotas.*" Henry borrowed the office Vespa and went up the road to see the damage, which wasn't all that great; then went back to the office to write up the insurance report. "Never mind the Civil Guard," Gomez said. "They've been told already. They'll do bugger all." There was the usual Monday-morning panic on in the typists' room and a spate of telegrams from Head Office. No one had seen Santiago, though.

"I had the word the Old Man's coming down."

"What old man?" Henry looked up.

"*The* Old Man. Martorell, Senior. Our Santi'd better pull his finger out, if you ask me."

El Sol of Malaga rang up to ask if it was true, so other people had the word, too. Henry, however, had no comment. There was nothing official, yet. In the architects' office things were relatively quiet, the main topics of conversation being Hanna Petrie's new bikini and Hanna Petrie's new bikini's contents. Gomez and Lopez Bravo thought that Our Santi had managed to get his end in there the previous night; Pepe Valderama wasn't so sure. Henry, again, had no comment. Back in his own office, there was another 'phone call. Someone had driven his Porsche into a stone wall and wanted to know who he could sue for damages. Our Santi was the office legal expert, but Our Santi wasn't in that morning. Our Santi would ring back as soon as he got in. Henry promised that he would, anyway.

A little before lunch another bunch of telegrams arrived, and the typists' room filled with a noisy excited chattering like that of a flock of disturbed starlings. It was true, then. The Old Man was coming down. Someone rang through to report the comings and goings of motor-cyclists around the van Koons' villa on the Saturday night. ("*Si, tipico, tipico.* Now they tell us.") There was also talk about some kind of an explosion up in the hills. People had been killed, but nobody knew who or how. It could have been the same lot—that seemed to be the point. Local yobs. Then just on one o'clock the bar at the Maritime Club reported that they'd run out of beer. The truck hadn't come

It all added up to pretty much of an ordinary Monday morning.

Henry got a lift down to Los Boliches for lunch. It was a hotter day, even, than yesterday. At the Santa Cruz bar, Cipriano was eating peanuts.

"Ramona wants to see you."

"When?"

"Tonight. Seven o'clock. In the Paseo, the bullring end."

"Both of us?"

"No. Just you."

He had a newspaper in front of him, open at the football page. The usual *Gran Victoria*, Henry noticed, for the home team. Away teams never had a *Gran Victoria*, except of course in their own local newspapers. The best they could hope for was a *Ganancia Oportuna*, a lucky win. Henry felt in rather an away-team mood that morning.

"Is there anything wrong?"

"Not that I know of," Cipriano said.

Henry ordered a beer, and sat drinking it while Cipriano read the newspaper and said nothing.

"It went off."

"Yes," Cipriano said. "It went off." He turned over the page. "Nothing in the paper, though. How did you hear?"

"The office. People were talking. No one seemed to—"

"Late last night. I haven't been able to find out much, either. But there was someone in there, all right."

"Who?"

"Two bodies. Almost certainly our friends with the motor-bike. But I don't know. It won't be easy to identify them."

He read another paragraph. Henry drank more beer.

"Tomorrow," Cipriano said eventually, "or the day after. Or maybe the day after that. Then they'll print a couple of names, and their ages in brackets, and where they came from. That's all there'll ever be, Henry. Nothing. Next to nothing. Just forget about it."

"Yes, but for tomorrow night ... we have to think of something better."

Cipriano put down the newspaper and looked for a while at his own reflection in the bar mirror. For the first time, the idea had occurred to him that this boy might be good. *Very* good. In the end he shrugged—to himself, and hence theatrically—and started to read the newspaper again.

Ramona was there before him, in the Paseo, but not until she was very close did Henry recognise her; not so much because of the way she was dressed as because of the way she was walking. Previously he had always seen her in plimsolls or in slippers, shuffling to and fro with a graceful yet top-heavy tilt; now she wore black shoes—of a kind that even Henry knew to be old-fashioned, with three-inch stiletto heels—and the change in her gait they effected was startling. Also, for Henry, a little unnerving. The large handbag she carried, which seemed to be heavy, in no way detracted from the flamboyance of her strut.

"I'm sorry," Henry said. "I didn't ... You look ..."

"I know. Don't say it."

She turned, affording him a brief glimpse of her spectacularly tight-skirted rump, and with one hand on his elbow guided him to the nearest gap in the palm-tree arboleda. Here, to the right of the main Paseo, were shaded sidewalks, bushes, bright-coloured flowers; there was heat but little sun, a jungle oppressiveness.

"Cipriano isn't coming."

"Don't worry about Cipriano," Ramona said.

There was a corner bar to the right, chairs, tables, a wooden kiosk, but they didn't go towards it. Instead they turned half left and started to walk slowly towards the town, Ramona's hand still resting in the crook of his elbow.

Henry found this a little embarrassing, but didn't like to protest.

"Yesterday, I told Cipriano something that I shouldn't have. I told him I was worried. I shouldn't have, but he knows me very well. He might have guessed."

"It was a flop," Henry said. "It didn't work. But I don't see—"

"No. It's not that."

"Then what?"

"Signs," Ramona said.

"Signs?"

"Yes. I believe in signs."

"You mean like ... walking under ladders?"

"Yes and no. I have a feeling. Something has gone or is going wrong. I can't say more than that."

"But what sort of thing?"

"I told you. I don't know. But there's only one thing that ever goes wrong, in the way I mean. Someone has talked."

"Who?"

"I don't know who."

"You're not saying, indirectly, that you think I've—"

She clicked her tongue. "I'm not an indirect person. I'm sure it's not you."

"Good."

"You're from another country, Henry. From another planet. You *could* have talked, certainly. But if you had, I wouldn't know. I wouldn't feel it. I trust you because I don't know you. I suppose that sounds odd."

"Ramona, I don't believe in *any* of this."

"That's why I can tell you. Because you won't believe it. Cipriano does, you see."

"But if it's not you or me, then it has to be Cipriano."

"I hope very much that it isn't Cipriano."

"But it could be?"

"Yes. It could be."

"It's ridiculous."

"It's unlikely."

"Well, but who else could it be?"

"Any one of many."

"*Many?*"

"There aren't just three of us, you know, working on this job. We three are just the spearhead. But there are many others. Many."

"But these others—do they know all about it?"

"Some more than others," Ramona said.

They were passing a wooden bench. Henry gestured towards it. "Should we sit down?"

"No," Ramona said. "We'll keep walking."

So they kept on walking.

"We have our informants, Henry. Because they're necessary. But the trouble with informants is that they can inform other people. Like the man who told us where and when Hernandez would be meeting Martorell. Nowadays, when we go after something, we never think that there *may* be a trap at the end of it ... We assume that there is, as a matter of course. We have to take the cheese and go away again. That's why we have all this business with the telephone. Otherwise, there'd be simpler ways. Much simpler. But that's how it is—there are many of us. But not so *very* many. Each one of us is valuable."

"I hadn't realised that. Martin didn't tell me that."

"You must try and remember it. You see, you're especially valuable, Henry, because you're a foreigner. You have no idea what an advantage that is. With us, they can do what they like. But with foreigners, they have to be more careful. They have to pause and think, and they don't like doing that. They're not good at thinking. They're intuitive—like me. In a way we understand each other very well—we and the Secret Police. For the last thirty years we've been fighting a draw. It's people like you who can break the deadlock, Henry—people that neither we nor the police can really

107

understand. That's what Martin's job is in England—to look for people like you. Otherwise, there'll be no end to it. It'll go on for ever."

Leaving the side paths, they stepped out on to the grey pavement and angled sunlight of the Alameda, the Post Office buildings to their left, the gardens of the Alkazar on the steep slope before them. It gave Henry a strange sensation of having broken cover. They crossed the road, through a gap in the evening procession of drifting cars, and turned sharp left along the pavement that skirted the high stone wall. "Where are we going? To your shop?"

"I have no shop," Ramona said. "I shan't be going there again."

"But the jelly?"

"Cipriano has it. It's safe."

"Oh," Henry said.

"Tomorrow afternoon, I shall take a train. My part in the job will be over. Tomorrow night, when you and Cipriano are hard at work, I shall be a couple of hundred miles from here. That's if all goes well."

"So I won't see you again?"

"After this, no. I'll explain to you what to do when *your* job is over. I'll give you a ticket. Wednesday morning, you'll be back in England. No—we won't be seeing each other again."

Now they were climbing the slope that led up to the Cathedral. It was Henry's impression that her grasp on his elbow had tightened very slightly; perhaps she found the slope a little tiring. He slackened his pace.

"We'll go to a house," Ramona said, "where they let rooms. Bedrooms. By the hour. That is the safest place for us to be. Because if anything happens there, Henry, you'll know what to tell them. You've got your passport?"

"Yes."

"Good. Always carry your passport. When they see it, they have to pause and think. They don't like that—as I told you. You can say that I spoke to you back there in the Paseo—which is the right place for speaking to strange men—and then we went to this place together. With any luck they won't even detain you." She sounded like a mistress at a finishing school, explaining some mysterious point of Continental etiquette. "Unless, of course..."

"Unless what?"

"Unless it *is* Cipriano."

Henry found himself, for some strange reason, compelled to take all this quite seriously. "But surely they're bound to think it very odd."

"I don't see why. I'm not so very ugly. There are plenty uglier than me in the business, I promise you."

"I didn't mean that at all. I meant, you're *not* in the business. So why should you—"

"But I am. I have a license. I'm registered. You didn't think I could make a living out of that bloody chemist's shop, did you?"

"I hadn't thought about it, really."

"It won't help *me* at all, if they're following us now. But it might help you."

"Yes," Henry said. "I see." There seemed to be quite a number of things that he hadn't realised. And this, in particular, didn't seem right. He felt mildly shocked.

In fact, the room wasn't in any way unpleasant. It wasn't sordid and it certainly wasn't voluptuous, though the light had a pink shade and was decidedly dim. It wasn't really anything other than functional; almost severely so. There was a wardrobe with a long mirror, not unlike the one in his room at Torrevedra; there were two wooden chairs and a small table; and there was, of course, a bed. Rather narrow, one would have thought, but with nice clean sheets. Henry, who had visualised it all rather differently, was relieved, though hardly put at ease.

"Phew," Ramona said.

Turning, he saw that she was unbuttoning her blouse. It was very hot, certainly. The one tiny window was shuttered. She pulled the blouse down from her shoulders and draped it over the back of one of the chairs, then began to unzip her skirt. "Better get undressed."

"You want me to . . . ?"

"For God's sake." But she sounded bored, rather than irritated. "If the cops come round, they won't bother to knock."

"You don't really think they will, do you? You said it'd be safe here."

"I said it'd be safe for *you*. Reasonably so. But you've got at least to look as if you've been putting it in. You bloody men always stick together." Even unzipped, the skirt was too tight; she was struggling, while she spoke, to drag it down past her haunches. The waistbelt had left a deep pink crease, Henry noticed, in the soft flesh above. ". . . Apologise to you, likely as not, for spoiling your evening's entertainment. That's been known to happen. Spanish hospitality, you know. Big, big deal. They give special courses to these girls at the tourist night-clubs—the customer's always right, provided he's a foreigner. Remember to arch your backs, my dears, keep the kind gentlemen's balls off the wet sand. *Ahhhhh* yes." The skirt at last collapsing round her ankles. "God, that thing was killing me."

She sat down on the bed and kicked off her tight black shoes, each in turn, then wiggled her toes in contentment. "Maybe you overdo it a bit," Henry said.

"You think so?"

Henry turned away, loosening his shirt. He pulled it up and over his head, while behind him the bed squeaked plaintively. Trousers, too? But surely *she* wasn't . . . Undress, she'd said. So trousers too, then. But what . . . ? Oh yes. Shoes first. Of course. That was stupid. He sat, badly

110

tangled, down on the chair and tugged at his shoelace. It snapped. *Damn.* "People don't usually complain," Ramona said.

"I wasn't complaining. I mean if it's ... part of the act..."

"Men don't like subtlety, you know. Not round here, anyway. Do they anywhere? Do they in England?"

"I suppose not. I don't really know." He held the shoe balanced for a moment in his hand, then dropped it. *Drop the other shoe,* there was a joke about that. But he couldn't remember it. Surely that had been a joke, too, about the wet sand? And ... subtle, no, that she certainly wasn't. She seemed a different woman tonight. Brassily cheerful. Not to say vulgar. Anyway, he'd never understood the Spanish admiration for women with very white skins; they seemed to him pasty, unhealthy; the plump ones reminded him of slugs. Ramona was plump.

He saw, turning back again, that she hadn't yet taken off her bra or her panties, which was a relief; it meant he could keep his underpants, presumably. She had the bag open on the bed beside her and was riffling through its contents. "This is your ticket, Henry. Put it in your wallet." The Iberia flight from Malaga to London, leaving at eleven-thirty-five on the Tuesday night. He nodded and took it over to his jacket.

"There'll be a car waiting when you've finished the job. You know the Ribera corner?" He nodded again. "There on the right. Cipriano will drive you to the airport. Take a bag like this, if you like; no other luggage. An hour and a half should give you plenty of time, but you'll have to get away quickly or you'll run into a roadblock." His wallet in his hand, he watched her unhooking her bra. Black cotton, elastic and metal catches. "All very simple. You'll find the worst part will be waiting at the airport, especially if you get there the best part of an hour early.

But just sit down and wait. Don't get nervous. And don't miss your flight. *Entendido?*"

"Yes," Henry said.

"Good."

"But what I wondered was ... Couldn't I stay?"

"Stay?"—as though she hadn't understood the word.

"Yes. They won't have any means of knowing it was me. Or Cipriano. We could just sit tight. Whereas if I run away—they're bound to guess.."

She was lighting a cigarette; the skin beneath her eyes pale and puffy in the match-flame, the fingers—competent, delicate, as always—shaking out the used stem. Her breasts moved also against the white squatness of her half-reclined body, quivered and settled as the match snapped out; the nipples were dark and flat, like old coins. Fascinated, Henry looked away.

"Sitting tight—that isn't as easy as it sounds. People don't trust you that much yet, Henry. People don't know you well enough. Better—much better—to play it safe."

"Who do you mean by *people?* Martin?"

"People," Ramona said.

She said nothing else, so Henry looked at her again. He had only half-heard her, anyway; there had been voices, other voices, in the next room. In the architects' office, Gomez, Valderama, what a pair, eh, *chiquito* ... ? what a set, and the low unsatisfied grunts of male laughter; Hanna, ha-ha, Hanna. At the party, with Santi's arm round her, his fingertips just touching them; big, they had to be big, big like these. Ramona's. But why, *why* ... ? I don't know. There's something wrong with me. There has to be.

"We don't want them to catch you, Henry. Not this time. Don't worry. You'll be back."

"We don't want them to catch you, either. Or Cipriano."

"You're different."

"Why?"

"I don't know. You're imaginative. That's probably it."

The cigarette glowed sharply above that sprawled and fluid whiteness. "That's the real trouble with this country. No imagination. People here see only what they're shown. It's the same in sex as in everything else—it all has to go in the window. We're halfway to being impotent, if you ask me. We're caught in a deadlock. I've thought about it, you know, I've thought about it a lot. We all do. It's our lives we're risking. So I think, and I think, and I think. But can I find any answers... ? No. I can't."

She laid down the cigarette in an ashtray. Her fingers—delicate, competent—patted the bed.

"Come and sit down, Henry. Come and sit here."

But why, why?

And knowing why all the time. That was the worst of it.

"I can't. I won't."

His hands were hard-clenched on stiff linen; the length of his body rigid and trembling. Ramona's shoulder was smooth and slippery with sweat against his cheek. The muttered cry, as though unheard by her; still she fought him, grimly, silently, as an angler steers his salmon towards the bank, her fingers moving up and down, up and down, always competent, always careful, clean white nurse's fingers, readying him for the operating table. Against his mouth, the anaesthetic pad of her neck, her yielding flesh. *Oh yes you can. You will.*

The voices, always the voices. From the other rooms. The corridor and the soundless wheels of the trolley. Other doors, white-painted; other rooms. Each with its narrow bed, its pink-shaded light. Creakings, moans, protestations; the white arches of lifted legs, reared in the plunging darkness. This was where it ended. The Accident Ward.

The steam, rising from the engine. The long dark tunnel. The voices, the others, the other women; the whores, the bitches he goes with. You won't understand, you can't.

You're too young, Henry. But one day you'll know what all these years I've had to put up with. "Oh God. No. *No*. It's no good."

No, she'd said, no. We can't go on. No no no no no. The words, the protestations, becoming inaudible behind the white door, the white-painted door with the twisted handle; no no no, we can't go on, there's nothing left, (the shrill accented voice changing in tone, rising in desperate denial,) no, I can't, I won't (the echoes of that denial reverberating in his lowered head, mingling with his own perplexed refusal to believe, *no, no, don't, she's the enemy, she's the others*) and the cold light of the headlamps startling him as he crouched, bewildered, in the dark-carpeted passage, the roar of the motor, the sharp reflected light streaming in through the half-open window at the head of the stairs so that he saw the leap of his own dressing-gowned shadow—gigantic, contorted—as he turned away; hearing, as he turned, blended with the rumble of the lorry that other sound, open-throated yet no longer shrill, low yet penetrating. Stop, oh stop. That noise. "Stop it. Stop it."

And the fingers at last pausing. Holding him calmly, motionlessly. "What noise?"

Henry's mouth was still wrenched open in an agonising rictus; sweat tickled his chin. He brought up his hand to wipe away the moisture, the movement freeing his jawlock; what noise? What did she mean? What noise? "I can't hear anything." He lifted his head, listening.

"You said, stop that noise."

"Did I?"

Up on one elbow. His back flexed, losing its rigidity; he was streaming with perspiration. Not just his face and neck; his whole body. Ramona, watching him; the fish diving for the deep bottom, for its covert of shimmering weeds. The fight was over. "It's no good," Henry said. "Is it?"

"It's too damned hot," Ramona said.

Broken bottles. Rusted tins. The bra looped over the arm of the chair, black elastic, crumpled black cotton. The sand, the hot sand. And the blue towel. Henry closed his eyes against the sun.

Nothing wrong, is there?

No. I don't think so. Nothing.

"I don't believe it. You made it all up—that about the police. Just to get me here."

This, to a corpse. Naked. Her eyes open but sightless, focused on a point somewhere beyond the ceiling. Her hands, also opened, rested on the crumpled sheet. "Look at me," Henry said. "You might at least *look* at me."

"I thought you'd rather I didn't," Ramona said. Her eyes didn't move. She raised instead her right hand, let it fall tiredly on the heavy curve of her stomach.

"You made it all up. Didn't you...? All that about somebody having talked. Nobody's talked. I don't believe you. You just wanted to... But why...? *Why?*"

"It was maybe a mistake."

"You admit it, then? You admit it was all lies?"

"It doesn't matter. None of it really matters. Let's just say perhaps I made a mistake."

Massaging gently the muscles there.

"Oh, you made a mistake all right. You certainly did."

But he didn't feel as angry as might have been expected. Disgusted, yes; with himself, as much as with her. And indignant. Supposing it had been all right, that wouldn't have made any difference—she was a liar, that was the point. Like all the others. That was why he wasn't angry; it was what he had expected. "I knew it all the time. Suspected it, anyway."

He buttoned his shirt, tucked it inside his trousers. Now her head turned on the pillow and she looked at him again;

grave, unsmiling. "Perhaps that's why it went wrong for you."

"Yes. That's why it went wrong." It was true. She had to admit it. A blowsy old bag, anyway. "Don't think I'm worried. I'm not worried. I'm just sorry you've been disappointed—that's all."

A stupid business. A hot, sweaty, sticky, stupid business. He picked up his jacket, swung it across his right shoulder. "There's no need for you to go," Ramona said.

"Why not? I've been here long enough, haven't I? For it to look good? You know—for those people who're waiting to pick you up." He shook his head, as if in despair at his own former gullibility. "God, it's all so stupid. And unnecessary."

"It needn't have been," Ramona said. "But you're right. It was a mistake. One shouldn't make mistakes."

Not being really angry, he was finding the outward show of anger, in an odd way, enjoyable. "Ought I to pay you something?"

"Don't be silly."

"Oh, all right. I'm sorry if I'm silly. I just like to be careful on these points of detail."

"Perhaps you *had* better go. Perhaps," Ramona said, "they are waiting for you to go." She closed her eyes. "Good luck, Henry."

"Thanks a lot. *Lo mismo digo.*"

He went out, closing the door behind him.

The passage outside was dim and airless. In it, he felt the nightmare returning, closing in on him quickly. Which way...? He could hear a radio playing, somewhere in the distance. No other sound. But then, as he listened, a host of tiny, unidentifiable sounds, furtive, hidden; he shook his head again, rejecting them, and started to walk. Which way...? Blank plaster walls, the dark-tiled floor; then a flight of stairs. He set off down them, trailing the back of one hand against the wall so that his fingernails brushed it lightly, maintained the weakest possible of material contacts. Ramona moved before him, a shiver of soft white flesh in the long mirror, strong hips and thighs; he descended open-mouthed, his tongue moistening his dry lower lip. At the foot of the stairs the patio opened out around him, dark and shadowed. Empty. No one about; no light left burning. The door...? There was no door. Nothing but white arches and, beneath them, darkness.

Later he found himself lying there, under the arches; curled up, his knees pressed against his chest, and with a taste of vomit harsh at the back of his throat. The ceiling, low and curved, slipped to and fro above him like a giant eyelid, the tracery of shadows throbbing there like veins. Yet somehow he managed to rise and to pull her also to her feet, holding her in turn imprisoned while his fingers scaled her upthrust bodies conjoined, hovering vertiginously over the swirling mirror-water that rose towards them, suck and pull of the tide dragging them down, then the gritty underwater blindness of the smooth-ribbed sand and the circling cry of the seagulls reverberant overhead as she fought him off, flurrying hands and wildly jerking buttocks, the green weeds of her eyes vacant with terror, then the shudder and liquid roll of her melon-shaped breasts as she swung across him, straddled him, and *this*, he thought, now *this, this,* his belly contracting again in sudden violence and the hot flow burning again through his nose and throat. Curled up on the stone floor of the patio, his fingers bent like claws, his eyes screwed shut. Thinking, *no, I'm alone and for ever alone; only this, the darkness, and sleep. But sleep I'm afraid of. In my sleep they wait for me, wide-eyed and naked; in a nest of tangled blankets, in a hut where a candle burns. I'll never sleep again...*

(he thought in his dream).

Later still, and as a part of the dream, there were footsteps and voices, the rattle of bolts, the creak of an opening door. From somewhere, a soft light that nonetheless pained

his eyes. He slept, and when he woke again they were crossing the patio; a small, grey-haired woman dressed in black
and behind her, just behind her, three men, walking erect
and very silently; one man in a grey suit, two men in uniform with polished boots. They paused at the foot of the
stairs for no more than a moment, then, one by one, began
to mount them. He could sense cool air from the open
door. Slowly, on hands and knees, he crawled towards it.

"There was a car?"

"A black car. I couldn't see the make."

"But not a police car? Did you see the plates?"

"It looked like an ordinary car to me. She got in the
back. And it drove away. Does it make any difference what
sort of car?"

"Yes," Cipriano said.

"But they've arrested her all right. No doubt about that."

"Oh no. No doubt at all. And sooner or later, they'll
make her talk—there's no doubt about that, either. The
only question is how long it'll take them. That's why I
wanted to know what sort of a car."

"I don't understand," Henry said.

"Look, the chances are she's been pulled in by the local
police. That's what I'm hoping. If so, they'll have had
instructions from the Special Branch in Madrid. You say
they got her about two in the morning...? Right. They'll
have notified Madrid, and Madrid will be sending somebody. Car or train, and most probably train. He'll be on the
way now. But he won't get to Malaga much before ... say
two o'clock this afternoon. At the earliest. All the fuzz will
do meanwhile is hold her till he arrives. You get the
picture?"

"You mean it gives us a chance to rescue her?"

"Rescue her? What, the two of us? You must be barmy."

"But we ought to—"

118

"We ought to carry on, *hijo*, with what we're supposed to be doing. If we had any reason to suppose that she'd blown us, then we'd have to call it off. The whole damned thing. But with any luck, she hasn't. And won't. She's got a time-limit. She knows it. And the police almost certainly don't. So things could be worse.'

Though not very much, Cipriano thought. Thinking straight was a major problem this morning; there was within him a strong desire to blame the whole bloody thing on Henry. But that was stupid. It hadn't been Henry's fault. "There aren't any buses from Malaga, are there?—after two in the morning. How did you get here?"

"I walked as far as the bridge and got a lift."

"You could have rung me."

"I wouldn't have known what to say. Not over the 'phone."

He was looking tired, very tired; that wasn't surprising. But not particularly nervous. Not for a man who'd had *that* narrow a squeak. "Cipriano—how did they know she was there?"

"I don't suppose they did. But they knew she was somewhere. So they checked the houses. That's one thing the buggers *are* good at," Cipriano said. "Give them some idea where to look for you, and nine times out of ten they'll find you. She knew that. Dam' stupid bitch."

"Stupid? Why?"

"Getting you mixed up in it like that. I can't think what got into her. You'd be in jug yourself right now, if you hadn't the luck of the devil."

It was easier, much easier to blame Ramona. And yet she'd been right. She'd had the "feeling" about herself, not about Henry. He imagined her sitting again at the bar in her white blouse and tight blue skirt, seeing the fatalistic countrywoman's lift of her shoulder; *que será, será*. She herself had been lucky, at other times. Now her luck had run out, and she'd known it.

The time limit was now their only chance.

When you're caught, they torture you, and when you're tortured, you talk. *Everybody* talks. Everybody knows it; you take it for granted. There's only one way to hold out for any length of time at all, and that's the same way you give up heroin. It's just about as easy. You don't say to yourself, *no, I'll never talk, I'll never tell them*. You say —or more likely, you scream—*yes yes YES! I'll tell you, I'll tell you everything. But first, I'll count up to a hundred*. And you start counting. Then in the eighties or the nineties, you say to yourself, *Well, I haven't told them anything so far. And if I've done it once, I can do it again.* Then it's one, two, three, four again, until the numbers dissolve in a mist of pain; and when you come to, you start all over again.

Like that, you can hold things up for a little while. No more than that. And later, you're surprised to learn how little a time it was.

But if you're really unlucky, you have a time limit which isn't decided by you yourself but by exterior circumstance. That was what Ramona now had to face. She had to last out till ten o'clock; if possible, till midnight. It *was* possible. Just. Six or eight hours can be managed; I know, because I've done it myself. And women take it better than men, as a general rule. You wouldn't think so. But they do. And people often waste time with women, raping them and so on. Well, it was possible. But very far indeed from being certain.

Still, it'd be the Special Branch. And I had the Civil Guard. The S.B. aren't so good at these physical things, because they're not so used to them. And it's mostly a matter of getting used to it; in the end, you don't even think of it as being cruel. It's just a job of work. Like a picador's. But till you're broken in to it, you have a problem; you don't get anywhere very fast if you have to go outside every five minutes to be sick. That's why I'd sooner have the Special Branch, myself—they're more the imaginative kind. The Civil Guard, they're stupid.

Ramona ought to last out. Just.

"But what if it wasn't a police car?"

"That'd mean that the S.B. are down here already," Cipriano said. He looked at his wrist-watch. Ten past six; enough light filtering in through the window for him to read the dial. "By now they'll have had four hours at her. And there'll be eighteen to go. We just have to assume that it *was* a police car. Otherwise, we haven't a prayer."

4

Coming down the slope, (the palomino side-stepping on the loose red earth, her right leg angled in the heavy triangular stirrup to hold the balance,) she reined in under the locust trees, where the shade was deepest; the sun was no more than an hour up, but already beginning to strike and the horse's flanks were polished dark with sweat. The algarrobos bunched on the twigs at shoulder-height were ready to fall; some, indeed, lay in the glossy dust beside the horse's hooves, hard and twisted like shrivelled, sun-blackened bananas. She reached across to break one from the branch; snapped it with some effort in two and chewed for a while on the bitter, leathery internal pulp. Beneath her was the valley, rock and ilex, arroyo and dirt track, all brightly lit by the spectacularly-angled sun; in the depths of the valley was the shattered debris of the shed, split timbers and broken planks thrusting up like broken teeth from the grinning brown-red gums of its soil foundations. She looked at it, without puzzlement, for some little time before remembering the office rumours, the newspaper reports; those blistered remnants seemed altogether natural to that hot harsh landscape, the devastation a part of the general dereliction of those crumbling hills. It excited no surprise, no speculation. But then she recalled the small single-column heading, the following lines of narrow smudged print; *explosion*; two people had died, had been killed down there beneath her, in the valley. How sad. How tragic. It was strange that the realisation did nothing to disturb her present mood of well-being, the early-morning euphoria engendered of the gallop up the stiff slope, the warm whip of the breeze, the rattling clamour of the hoof-beats; if anything, it enhanced it. She tossed away the husk of the fruit, spat out the masticated pulp; took a handkerchief from her pocket and wiped her mouth and fingers. She wore no make-up this morning, not even lipstick. *This is me*, she thought; *I'm here and I'm glad I'm alive.* The horse moved forwards again at the touch of her heels, head dipping as the sharp hooves slithered. It was odd, of course, if this should be happiness; no cool drinks, no high-powered sports car, no stereophonic sound; just being alone and hot and thirsty on a good horse, looking at a place where people had died. *Poor them*, yes. *But lucky me.*

Back once more in his room, Henry got the B.E.A. bag from the wardrobe and put it on the table and sat for a while, his chin in his hands, staring at it. He'd had no breakfast. He wasn't hungry.

Soon it would be time to go to work.

Later he took the Luger pistol from its drawer and sat with it in his hands, moving the breech-bolt to and fro, to and fro. The action was a little stiff but the clicks were smooth, mechanical. Everything should be like that. Everything. Precision built. Of course, things would go wrong sometimes; you expected things to go wrong. No machine is perfect. But there was no need for this business of having *feelings* about it ... intuitions ... whatever you called them. He hadn't told Cipriano everything about last night. About Ramona. Naturally not.

At the end, he'd behaved badly. He knew it. He'd been taken out of his depth. Superstition is something you fight against, like all that predestination stuff; *it's got your number on it.* A lot of bollocks. He pushed the magazine back into the butt and laid the pistol down on the table. It was hot in his little room, it was always hot there now, and he felt tired, yet with no inclination to sleep. Half past seven, his wrist-watch said. He stood up and fetched from the drawer where the Luger had lain an old newspaper, slightly besmirched with oil; then began to collect his things—his tanks, his aeroplanes, his model soldiers—wrapping each one in a torn-off sheet of newspaper before packing it away carefully in the bag. There wouldn't be room there for them all. He'd take only the best.

This was a good one. A Stadden Gribeauval; a French 12-pounder, used in the Napoleonic Wars. Unpainted, of course. You saw the detail better that way. And this was Napoleon himself, mounted on his charger. Designed by Marcus Hinton, hand-cast and trimmed. The young Napoleon, not the Waterloo model. He'd been twenty-seven years old at the time of the battle of Mondovi ... though battle you could hardly call it. An action, perhaps ... ? perfectly planned, brilliantly executed. And this one...?

No. A clockwork drummer. You wind it up and put it on the table and then it beats a tattoo; not just any old rattle, but a proper military tattoo. It could stay behind, though. On the whole, one doesn't go in for working models. They're rather frowned on. What you want is simplicity and perfection of detail. That's what Napoleon himself always aimed at. Of all possible choices, the simplest. The direct line.

Henry turned the key a few times and set the drummer down on the floor, where it vibrated to the metallic clatter of the tiny metal pans. Half past seven; fifteen-odd hours to go. The key unwinding slowly in the shuddering red-painted back, the spring unfolding. We're all motivated, aren't we?—in our different ways. That's not to say we're puppets. It's all in the key, the key to the clockwork. Of all choices, the simplest. *The direct line*. Henry stared at the quivering toy on the floor, seized by a new and unusual excitement; he had the sensation that he himself was quivering all over, trembling to the impact of his idea. The direct line, the simplest of all; and that of course was the answer. Why hadn't he thought of it before? Why hadn't Cipriano?

The scarlet-coated toy stuttered to a halt. Henry stooped to pick him up. A final brief spasm; *tock-tock-tock.* And then it was ended. Henry dropped the drummer once more to the floor, ground him to pieces under his heel. He packed the rest of his more valuable pieces away, quickly and competently, and placed on top of them the Luger pistol; zipped shut the bag. That was it. He was ready to go.

Walking past the hotel, stepping a little clumsily in her unaccustomed riding-boots, she heard her name being called and, stopping and turning, saw him coming down the hotel steps, taking them three at a time, his black hair flopping loosely over his furrowed brown forehead. "Well, *you're* up early," she said.

"Busy day ahead. Where've you been?"

"Out riding." It had to be obvious.

"Last night, I meant." He came to a halt in front of her, pushing his hair back with his right hand; he certainly seemed to be more than usually harassed. "I tried to call you. Wondered if you were doing anything this evening."

"This evening . . . ? Nothing."

"Papa's coming down. As you know. Today."

"Yes. We know."

"Cooking up some kind of a business deal or other. The thing is he'll be dining with me afterwards, up in my flat. Ruggiero's laying on something special. Well, and I wondered if you'd like to come, too."

"To meet your *father?*"

"For dinner. Yes. Just the three of us."

An extraordinarily diffident approach, for Santi. All the same she wasn't far off panic. The velvet red would be all right, surely; but her *hair,* she'd been *riding,* God.

125

There'd be time, though. Just. For an emergency appointment. And this was an emergency, if ever there was one. To meet his ... "God, you might have asked me before."

"I did, I mean I *tried,* I told you. But the bloody office 'phone wasn't working. And I wasn't even sure if ... Anyway, you can come?"

"Yes, I'd like to."

"Nine o'clock, then. At the flat."

"De acuerdo."

Maybe not the red velvet, though. Too low a neckline. Inviting you to dine with Papa, that has to be serious. The black might be safer. Santi smiling, squeezing her elbow, walking away. That was more like the old Santi; *nine o'clock at the flat*; the royal command. Still, there it was. Dinner with a millionaire, Anita baby. A good, good day, right from the start.

She watched him heading for the office with long, quick, characteristically nervous strides. A busy day ahead. She'd have to be quick, too; the hairdresser would need at least an hour, probably two. But that was Santi all over. Last-minute Santi, everything on impulse. Being rich, you got away with it. And anyway, what was wrong with doing things on impulse? You didn't have to plan and work out and worry at everything in life, for God's sake. There he went, striding towards the office, swinging open the door, almost colliding as he went in with ... who was it? ... Good Lord. Henry. Last-moment Santi and Henry Head-in-Air, what was it he'd dropped? It looked very like a luncheon-bag. Almost certainly a luncheon-bag. And that was Henry all over, when you thought about it. Coffee and sandwiches at the office desk. That was about his mark. Dinner at the flat with Santi's father, something rather special from Ruggiero; that was another proposition, however you looked at it. And besides...

She turned away and walked on down the pebble path that skirted the hotel, frowning at her own booted feet. Right now she didn't much want to think about Henry.

"What you got in there? A machine-gun?"

"Ha-ha," Henry said.

But Santiago wasn't, in point of fact, in a mood for badinage; his conversation with Anita had reminded him that not everything in the office was in order, and today it was important that it should be. "My damned telephone's on the blink."

Henry swung the blue B.E.A. bag from one hand to the other; it had certainly gone down with a hell of a clunk. He hoped nothing was damaged. "The one in your office?"

"Of course I mean the one in my office. Get hold of Cipriano. I want it fixed."

"Right away," Henry said.

But right away would of course have been too soon. Henry signed for the office Vespa and spent an hour puttering to and fro before heading down the village to Cipriano's office. His mood of excitement had passed; he felt tired, tireder than before, and slightly thick-headed. But the idea he'd had was still a good one.

"Why don't we use the direct line?"

"What direct line?" Cipriano, one would have said, felt slightly thick-headed, too.

"Santiago's line. The one from his flat to his office."

"Is there one?"

"He uses it every morning, or damned nearly. It's by his bed. He doesn't even have to get up."

"Wait a minute."

Cipriano opened a drawer in his desk and took out a file of wiring diagrams. "I had these out yesterday. But I didn't see ..."

127

His office was a rented room off the main street in Fuengirola. It was hideously noisy. The noise of the passing traffic beat on Henry's ears like surf.

"... Yes. You're right. But the flat...? How do we get there?"

"Break in, if we have to. It only has to be for a few minutes. And if we do that, we don't have to worry about an observation post. We can kill two birds with one stone. You can see everything that goes on in the offices from his flat ... I know. I've been up there."

"Into *his* office?"

"Yes. Perfectly. Unless, of course, they draw the blinds."

"Even if they do," Cipriano said, "we'll have the binoculars. We'll see their shadows. And besides, it'll be hot tonight. They won't draw the blinds. If we can see just when to do it—"

"And we'll have the 'phone right there to hand."

"Direct line. No dialling brushes, no switchboard. Nothing to go wrong at all. We lift the auricular, press the button and *bing*o. I like it, Henry. I like it."

"It's better than our first idea. It's so simple."

"And as you say ... two birds with one stone." Cipriano gave a little choking gurgle of suppressed laughter; the excitement that Henry had felt was now reaching him. "I like it. It's good."

"Then we'll do it?"

"I don't see why not."

He flipped the folder shut, put it in the leather work-case that stood open on the floor at his feet. The excitement still bubbled—"Yes. Yes, we'll *do* it"—but carried an undercurrent of uneasiness. Why hadn't *he* thought of it? It was there, it was all there in the wiring diagrams. He'd looked at them. He'd missed it.

He had to be slipping.

"The place'll be empty, won't it...? It's a proper doddle."

"I should think so, with the old man arriving. He'll be down at the office to meet his father—that's for sure."

Well, not quite for sure. But either way, (Cipriano thought,) it hardly mattered.

"We'll set it up this afternoon. After the siesta. I should get some sleep, if I were you. You'll probably need it."

It was true that Henry's eyes were sore. He rubbed them with his knuckles as he stood up.

"No news of ... ?"

"No," Cipriano said. "No news at all."

The Comisaría. Passages with frosted glass doors; offices with tray-laden desks and with tall filing cabinets; other files —row on row of them—on shelves and stacked on the floor, picking up dust. Here in Malaga there were high windows giving on the Alameda and canvas screens to trap the cool sea air; it was brighter and pleasanter, perhaps, than the grey stone building in East Madrid, just off the Rio Rosas, but cop shops are much the same all the world over. Bellido didn't much like the Rio Rosas precinct, where he usually worked, and he didn't much like this one, either—there was always the same atmosphere of weary officialdom, and the Special Branch is nowhere popular. Oh, they were polite enough in Malaga, but they didn't really want to know.

Still, they'd got the call through. That was something.

"We have your contact, *mi coronel*. The car passed through Andujar twenty minutes ago."

"Better stop them in Cordoba," Bellido said.

"That won't be necessary. We've made the call direct. Señor Martorell has a telephone in his car." The operator had one of those irritating know-it-all voices; the girl on the Rio Rosas switchboard was just the same. "He's waiting to speak to you now."

"Then why the hell didn't you say so?"

"I'll put you through," the girl said, sounding this time slightly injured.

A telephone in his car. Bloody marvellous. Bellido had been called up at four in the morning to grab a train from Principe Pio at four-forty-five a.m.; they hadn't told him much then and they'd told him nothing since. He hadn't an official car for his own use, let alone one with a telephone in it. But then he was only a Colonel in the Special Branch. As they said down here, *cazi ná*. The receiver in his hand crackled quietly ."*Oiga? ... Oiga? ...*"

And after some twenty seconds, behind the whisper of static, another voice.

"*Martorell habla.*"

"Colonel Bellido here. Of the Special Branch. I'm calling you from the Comisaría here at Malaga."

"Yes," the voice said, acknowledging the introduction, expressing no curiosity. It was only just audible. The line wasn't good.

"We understand you're at present travelling down to Malaga, Señor Martorell, and continuing to Torrevedra. We've some reason to be concerned as to your safety." It was always better to use the same old official phrases. *Someone's going to kill you*—that's over-dramatic. "Ice," the voice replied.

"I beg your pardon?"

"I said, that's nice. But that's what the police are for. To protect private citizens and their property. Why bother to tell me?"

"It seemed proper to warn you. An arrest has, in fact, been made. We hope we'll get further information as a result, but..."

"Yes. I know. I've heard that word before."

"What word?"

"*But.*"

"We'll do our best, sir. You can rest assured on that point."

"What do you want me to do?" the voice said patiently.

"The best thing of all—if my advice isn't presumptuous —would be for you to cancel your trip and return to Madrid."

"That is not possible."

Meaning that he didn't choose to. Bellido gnawed at his lower lip thoughtfully. "Well, no doubt you'll have taken the normal precautions?"

"I have my bodyguard with me, if that's what you're hinting at."

"Good. Good. But we'd like to give you an additional escort to your destination. You'll have no objection?"

The voice said nothing.

"... *Oiga? ... Oiga? ...*"

"I've no objection," the voice said.

"Then you'll be joined just before you reach Malaga, at the bottom of the Cuesta de la Reina. According to our information, you're travelling in a black Mercedes, registration number M 15683. Can you confirm that?"

"Correct."

"Thank you. I'll be in touch if there's any further news."

"Muy bien."

The telephone clicked in Bellido's ear.

Twenty minutes out of Andujar, he thought. Driving through the Sierra de Cordoba, at three o'clock on a blinding hot summer day. It wasn't surprising if the old man felt short-tempered; it was a dry, exhausting journey. Bellido knew that. He'd just done the trip himself.

The rest of the day was likely to prove even more exhausting. A lot of time had been wasted already; ten minutes more or less wouldn't make any difference. Ten minutes was the time he needed to roll and smoke a cigarette. He rolled one. He smoked it. He tried, as always on these occasions, to concentrate on the sweet, biting flavour of the black tobacco, to savour the sting of the smoke at the back of his palate—to enjoy, in a word, the cigarette

131

without thinking any more about the task immediately to hand. In this he didn't succeed. He never did. When he had finished he got up, and walked out of the room and down the passage, past the sign painted on the wall that said SALAS DE INTERROGACION and through the soundproof door beyond. There were three interrogation rooms in the Comisaría at Malaga. All of them were much too large. An interrogation room should be very small indeed.

The enquiry, of course, had already started. It had begun punctually at midday, in accordance with telephoned instructions from Madrid. These had been re-transmitted through the proper official channels and finally passed on, for action, to Sergeant Valdes. As far as Valdes was concerned, these were orders like any others; he was a little grizzled man with a deeply-lined face; he knew that for everything that happened there was a reason and he had seen, twenty-odd years ago in Morocco, what some of those reasons were. He was not a sadist. He had simply been in the Political Branch for a very long time. However, he hadn't met Bellido before. He straightened up when the Colonel came in and saluted; the Colonel was in civilian clothes, but if he didn't rate a salute he had no right to be there. "Sergeant Valdes," the Colonel said, to show that he had.

"Yes, sir."

"Colonel Bellido."

"Yes, Colonel."

"I'll examine the prisoner."

"*A la orden.*"

The prisoner lay on a rough canvas sheet on the padded interrogation table. The leather thong had been buckled loosely round her neck, but her arms and legs were free, as was the usual practice. Valdes knew the rulebook, if nothing else. Bellido swung his left hip over the table and perched himself beside the prisoner; picked up one dangling wrist and checked her pulse rate. "Has the doctor given her any drugs?"

"Not yet, Colonel. He says she's in excellent health."

Bellido nodded, and lowered the wrist again. He leaned forwards to examine the prisoner's face more closely, and saw, from under the lowered half-moons of eyelids, his gaze sedately returned. Always an interesting moment, this—the confrontation of adversaries. That calm, unenquiring stare told him that his arrival had been expected. Valdes had worked conscientiously, had caused great pain and no serious damage—at least by the standards of the rulebook—but the prisoner had known all along that the real opponent, the Grand Inquisitor, would be coming and had contrived to keep a main reserve of strength in hand. The prisoner probably knew a great deal. An old hand, certainly. Yes.

Interesting.

"Colonel Bellido," Bellido said.

The eyelids flickered. The prisoner would have trouble in speaking with her front teeth missing, but then the prisoner had no intention of speaking at all. That didn't matter. That was normal. Bellido would do the talking ... to start with.

"Would you like the Sergeant to bring you a glass of water?"

No reaction. None was expected. Bellido placed his hand gently on top of hers, his palm over the knuckles and reddened joints, just clear of the crushed and bloody roots where the fingernails had been. It might have been a caress. "I'm a policeman," Bellido said. "A public servant. My job is to try and prevent the loss of people's lives. I'm not a cruel man. Neither is the Sergeant here. We're not kind men, either. We have no strong feelings either way about you. It's just that, if you want, you can help us. We know that you can help us. And if you refuse to, then we must carry on trying to make you." His voice was soft, firm, persuasive; the voice of a very experienced primary school-teacher, exerting through the simplest of phrases an effortless dominance. His fingers maintained on the prisoner's hand a gentle, constant pressure, emphasising a physical contact; later, when in the toils of those surging throes of pain that resemble so surprisingly those of total sexual abandon, she would feel again the touch of his hand on hers and would remember his gentle voice, would turn to him, would trust him. From torturer and tortured to seducer and seduced is the simplest and most natural of steps. "Killing people solves no problems. It's foolish to persist. Remember that, at the very worst, you and your friends—if that's what they were—will go to prison. As to that, I can make no bargains with you. But prison is nothing. It's soon over. You're out and free. While death goes on for ever, and pain seems to. You're a brave woman— I can see that. You may think that it's brave to resist us for as long as you can. But it's foolish. It's very stupid. There's nothing to be gained by it. No one's death is really a gain. A death can only be a loss. You're going to suffer pain for nothing—very great pain. Far more pain than you've suffered up to now. And all so that somebody may die. Somebody who may, for all you can tell, drop dead of a heart attack tomorrow. Martorell isn't young. It could easily happen. In a word, it's a waste, Ramona—a wicked waste. *You're* young. If we have to go on, you may not die —it isn't my intention that you should die. You're young and you're attractive. As well as brave. But you won't be young and attractive two hours from now. You won't even, in any real sense of the word, be a woman any more. All you'll have left is bravery. Bravery, stupidity, however you look at it. It won't be enough, you know. It's all happened before. And it never is."

Her eyes were closed now. He waited for a few more seconds, then took away his hand. He stood up.

"I'm going to take a shower," he said to Valdes. "Then we'll begin. The wire brushes first."

"Yes, Colonel."

"You'd better get her stripped."

"Very good, Colonel."

"*Y nada de marranadas.* No messing about."

"Of course not, sir. *Nada de eso.*"

Valdes sounded quite shocked.

"You'll want water, sir? And a sponge?"

"It shouldn't be needed."

"It's customary, Colonel."

"Ah," Bellido said. "Then we'd better have it. Water. *And* a sponge."

Valdes nodded and saluted. He seemed a nice enough fellow, Bellido thought. Easily mollified.

Santi was like a cat on hot bricks.

"What the hell's the matter, Cipriano?"

"Not to worry," Cipriano said. "We fix."

"Yes, you fix, and bloody soon. Took your time getting round here, didn't you? That 'phone has got to be in order by nine o'clock. And that at the latest."

"Half an hour I need. That's all."

"Of course it has to be today the bastard goes dead. Ah, well. Get on with it."

This time it was going to be much easier. The telephone was on the desk and held in clamps. The thermos flask was right beside it. Cipriano, standing by the door, beckoned him in.

"All set?"

"Get on with it," Cipriano said.

Henry went to the desk and looked down at the 'phone. From then on, it was as though he was watching it all happen. His own fingers, steady and practised, on the flask-top, spinning on its thread; the fingers lifted it, placed it on the desk, then placed the inner plug gently beside it.

The narrow tilted circle of the Anglepoise lamp held the inverted cradle in its beam. Henry peered downwards, checking the position of the detonator; it might have been moved, that last time, when he'd poured in the jelly. But now it was wired and glued; it wouldn't shift. He checked it all the same.

Then the slow, glutinous trickle, the familiar smell rising, harsh in his nostrils. The flask in his right hand, the ribbed barrel ice-cold against his palm. From Cipriano, watching at the door, no sound. From the architects' office, no sound. From outside the open windows, no sound. There was sweat now on his forehead. The flask, almost empty, tilting. And now from the road, the sound of an approaching car, travelling fast; its engine revving as it came out of the turn. The last drops, slowly oozing. And that, what was *that* . . . ?

He listened for a moment.

No. Nothing. A globule of sweat was all, falling from his chin to the desk; *plip*. He couldn't have heard that, surely? Not possible. But he had. His hands were suddenly seized with a brief tremor, but now it didn't matter. The flask was empty.

The incendiary agent, packed in its transparent plastic bag; this time, the blue-edged flame of the explosion would be touched with silver, with the brightness of magnesium. A beautiful effect. He tested the firmness of the packing with one fingertip and lo, it was good; as neat a job as any he'd ever done. Now the telephone base with its sticky seal that would set in position; screw it down. Adjust. Then turn and turn. There.

Tight.

Now release the clamps. Steady fingers. Careful.

And over we go.

Right way up. Very slowly. Very gently. Holding your breath . . .

There.

He stepped back. Cipriano left the door to come towards him. *"Bien, chico, bien.* Leave the rest to me."

Henry replaced the plug and the cap of the thermos flask, put it back in Cipriano's open work-case. It was done now. He closed his eyes.

"Go on now. Get out of it. Half past eight—outside the hotel."

"Half past eight," Henry said. *"Hasta entonces."*

With no windows and no watches, time has very little meaning. And there's nothing there to look at, to focus the attention upon. That's why the room is always small. There's only the ceiling above you and part of one bare wall; even the lighting is indirect, nowadays. All this so that there can be no escape. In moments of extreme pain, as in those of spiritual ecstasy, the mind can leave the body and join itself to any other animate or inanimate body that may happen to be visible—a fly on the wall, the handle of a door, even some indeterminate patch of light or shade. And so there's nothing there, except the blank white ceiling and the blank white walls. There's nothing left but memories. Memories are what they want to get at. While the pain is vivid and if there's no escape, then the mind, too, has to become like a blank white wall; in the intervals, it grabs at memories as the lungs grab for air. Any memories at all, any images of the outside world; you have indeed no control over them. They simply come in a rich, warming flood and you stare at them with sightless eyes until the pain comes again.

This alternation of pure, near-hallucinatory recollection with pure, agonised sensation is what drives you mad. But they don't want that, either. So once in a while they give you their own faces to look at. There was a face poised above Ramona now and she knew that the face was real; a brown, alert face with slightly protuberant blue eyes and

137

with greying hair brushed back from the temples. The lips were held back a little, too, over white, even teeth, and there were thin creases etched into the skin at the corners of mouth and eyes, as though he were, at that moment, sharing in her pain or moving with her towards a sexual climax; there was effort in the face, excitement, exhaustion, and a strange kind of concern. Afterwards he'd say, uncertainly, *Well, was it good...*? And he said something to her now that she couldn't hear or couldn't understand but yes, she thought, *yes, do it to me*, remembered pain welling through her body, searing her hair and lips and thighs, *that, yes, that but no memories*, and with the thought the memory came of his turning away from her, reaching for his shirt, the smooth white skin below the line of suntan on his naked body touching her belatedly with lust, then nothing but the whiteness of the ceiling and the clammy warmth of her own sweat on the sheet beneath her, *it's hot, it's too damned hot*, and then the bucket of ice-cold water, smashing into her face and over her shoulders and breasts, lacerating like the stroke of a thousand razors, jerking her back to consciousness. She screamed, though now not loudly; a high-pitched, angry mewing, fierce as a seagull's. He'd turned away and had gone, had left her to the ice-water bucket and the hot kiss of the fish-hook, and now she couldn't even remember his name. He came from another planet; that was all she knew. And even that much she wouldn't tell.

"One name. Just one. That's all we need. Let someone else take his turn."

The voice was quiet and coaxing. She understood him now. She turned her head away from him a couple of inches, as far as she could, and blood came out of her nose in a trickling stream. One name. What name?

She couldn't remember.

*   *   *

138

The car was a Renault R10 four-seater, and it had been drawn up to the side of the road in the shade of a eucalyptus clump. The key, with a large label attached, was in the ignition lock. "It's just a hired car," Cipriano said. "No great mystifications. No business with numberplates. It's there, though, and that's the main thing."

"Did you think it wouldn't be?"

"The way things have been going, it's as well to be sure."

The sun had set now, and under the trees it was almost dark. The Ribera crossroads were set in a hollow; the topmost storeys of the hotel were visible above the steep crest to their right, while to their left a slower, gentler slope led the asphalted road past three sharp bends to the Petries' villa, to some smaller bungalows and then out on to the main road to Malaga. "Say four minutes," Cipriano said, "from Santi's flat to here. We drive off straight down the side road and circle to Los Boliches, say four minutes more. Then direct to Torremolinos and the airport. We ought to beat the cordon at Carvajal easily enough. No problem there. Getting out of the hotel will be the trickiest part."

He turned and looked back at the high, rectangular cliff of the hotel; the rows of open windows, the silhouetted parasols on the sun-roof and, perched on top, the flat, angular outline of the penthouse flat. "It shouldn't be too difficult," Henry said. "The foyer's always full of people coming and going."

"It's not so much the foyer. The lift's what I don't like. I've a thing about lifts. I wish there were some other way of getting there."

"There's a fire escape."

"We can't use that. Much too conspicuous."

They began to walk up the road towards the hotel. Cipriano went empty-handed, Henry carried his carefully-packed B.E.A. bag, full of toy soldiers. They had gone some thirty paces before it occurred to him that he could as easily have left it in the car; however it wasn't all that heavy. It didn't seem worth the trouble of going back.

"*Qué tal, amigo?*"

"I'm fine," Henry said, a little primly.

"So here we go."

"Here we go."

"And if it all goes well, tomorrow morning you'll be safe in London. Lucky sod. Telling Martin about it. And of course, if it *doesn't* go well . . ."

"I know what he'll say."

"Martin?"

"Yes. *Dulce et decorum est pro patria mori.*"

Cipriano slapped his shoulder lightly, almost with affection. "That's it. That's just what the old bastard *would* say. But it won't come to that. You're not such a bad sort, Henry . . . *por ser inglés*. We don't want to lose you." Then, after a pause, "In a way, that's the point. You *are* English. It isn't even your bloody *patria*."

"It's your country, yes. It's everybody's cause."

"That's a good way of putting it."

They reached the crest of the slope and stopped there for a moment, two small figures in the gathering night, the hotel looming high above them now, gigantic bulk of glass and concrete enveloping them in its shadow. For a while they looked up at it, together, in silence. The scent of flowers hung in the warm air; *damas de noche* on the garden walls. At their feet, the dust was faintly luminous. Cipriano said,

"I bet you don't know how that poem goes on."

"What poem?"

"That Latin one."

"I don't," Henry said, "as a matter of fact."

"Well, it says you may just as well die when your time comes along and put a good face on it . . . because even if you run away, they'll shoot you in the back. So there's no way of ducking out of it. Something in that, wouldn't you say?"

"Because it's your destiny, sort of?"

"Appointment in wherever-it-was."

"Samarra?"

"Yes. Samarra."

"I don't believe in it," Henry said.

"Nor do I. No. Not really. But Ramona did."

"Did?"

"Yes. Did. I suppose if you believe in it, *did* and *does* and *will do* are all much the same. An odd girl—Ramona."

He was, if it came to that, pretty odd himself. It was odd his knowing that poem, and about that book. But then Cipriano had read a whole lot more than you'd have thought. He was a thinking man. An *interesting* man, really. Henry would have liked (the thought came quite suddenly and unexpectedly) a long conversation with him; there'd been opportunities for that in the past—for long, nocturnal, philosophical chats, animated by a bottle of solera —but now they were gone. Perhaps something that now had brought them together had until this moment been lacking; a shared, tongue-loosening tension, a shared fear. But it was a pity. And besides, it couldn't be that. Henry wasn't afraid. He felt expectant, rather than tense. He felt fine.

He looked down at his wrist-watch. "A quarter to nine," he said; and Cipriano nodded.

"Right. Let's go."

The lift whispered quietly as, empty, it rose from its ground-floor station; whickered to a third-floor halt. Henry and Cipriano stepped inside. Cipriano pressed the top button and it rose again, hissing a little now at the extra weight. Cipriano unbuttoned his jacket. The butt of the revolver projected slightly from the spring-clip shoulder holster; he pushed it inwards, working it under his armpit. "That better?"

"Yes," Henry said.

"Ten to one he won't be there, anyway."

The steel snake of the cable unwound above them. Henry stared at the indicator panel above the door. Seven. Eight. Nine. The lift mounted smoothly, steadily, without vibration.

"Where's yours?"

"In my bag."

"Get it out."

Henry unzipped the bag and took out the Luger.

"God. That's a bloody cannon."

"It's the only one I've got."

He pushed it down inside the waist-belt of his trousers.

"It won't be needed," Cipriano said.

Henry leaned back against the metal panelling, feeling then the soft judder against his shoulders and the soles of his feet. He didn't like lifts, either. The number 14 winked amber, then went out. Cipriano reached for the door release catch.

Henry said,

"We're not too early?"

"We can't leave it any later. The old boy may get here ahead of time." A click. A stillness. The metal box was poised now over the long, hollow, echoing shaft, a hundred and sixty-odd feet of emptiness under their feet. "...And anyway. We're there."

He swung the door open, and they stepped out on to thick blue carpeting. Ahead of them was the narrow cream-painted passage, the door to the apartment. Cipriano turned to press the button, to send the lift whining downwards again. It left, as it sank, a faint reflected glow that faded to darkness; in the passage, though, a shaded lamp burned. They walked, shoulder to shoulder, towards the door, their feet sinking into the pile of the carpet as into damp humus. The Luger moved uncomfortably against Henry's stomach.

Cipriano touched the bellpush. From behind the door, they heard the sharp stridency of the buzzer; it stopped, cut off short, and there was no other sound. They waited, listening. In the end, Cipriano said. "Good."

He took from his pocket the mica strip, the wire picklock. Then, even as he began to stoop, Henry heard the click of turning wards, the rattle of the door handle. The door swung open. Santi, his shirt unbuttoned, towel draped round his neck, stared out at them.

"Yes?" Santi said.

The doctor came out of the interrogation room, drying his hands on a fluffy towel and making a little too much of a thing of it. He was a police doctor and he had visited interrogation rooms before; but a doctor is always a doctor first and foremost, and being a doctor is a very different thing from being a policeman. "I suppose this interrogation has to continue?"—wiping away like Pontius Pilate and not looking at Bellido when he spoke. They nearly always said something like that. And afterwards thought, well, I *did* protest. Bellido nowadays never made the mistake of giving an over-emphatic reply; there was no point in hurting anyone's feelings.

"I'm afraid so," he said.

"Yes. Well, I've given her a stimulant. Intravenal. It should keep her going for another hour or so. But from then on, her heart may give out at any moment. I'd advise some caution."

"Thank you," Bellido said. An extra hour was what you usually got; you never knew whether you hoped for longer or not. What you *really* wanted was to be done with the whole bloody business, one way or another; but of course, you couldn't say so. An hour can be a very long time. An hour can be very nearly eternity.

"There's that haemorrhage. That'll stand watching. She'll try to provoke it, naturally. If the blood gets down into her lungs, she'll choke to death very quickly. You'll know about that. But don't forget she knows it, too."

"No," Bellido said. "I won't forget."

The doctor nodded and walked away, still without having looked at him. Bellido, on the whole, preferred it that way. When you got a look, it was invariably one that said, *I wouldn't have your job for any money;* Bellido didn't like being pitied. No Spaniard does. And in fact there's precious little money involved, *amigo.* No money, no expense account, no sleek foreign cars with telephones. A second-class rail ticket took you out and when you got back, the priest would give you absolution; that was all that could be said for it. You fought your country's enemies, and no one wanted to know. Bellido sighed, and crushed out his cigarette, and went back into the interrogation room. The attendant had been in with his pail and his string mop, and the blood, the urine and the faeces had all been cleared up. Everything was neat and tidy. The doctor had gone and the sergeant was waiting. The prisoner, too, was waiting. The interrogation had to continue. Bellido took off his jacket and draped it over the back of his wooden chair; the prisoner raised her left knee maybe an inch. An involuntary movement. All her movements now were involuntary; her muscular control had gone. It was all of twenty minutes since she'd last screamed. But now the doctor had brought a little part of her back, just enough of her for the interrogation to continue.

"An hour has to do it, sergeant. Either way."

Valdes didn't nod. He knew already. And so, it was almost certain, did the prisoner.

"You were damned slow," Cipriano said.

Slow in answering, too. Henry had to swallow first. "I didn't..."

"It's no good thinking about it, you know. Talking about it. Just *do* it."

Henry's ears were still singing. He felt giddy.

"Give us a hand," Cipriano said.

"... You're going to move him?"

"We don't want him right in front of the door, do we? We may want to get out of here quickly. No harm in being careful."

He was stooping already over Santi's slippered feet. That left Henry with the shoulders. Between the two of them, it wasn't difficult; or especially unpleasant, except for when he first lifted and Santi's head lolled back loosely on its neck and a bubble of bright red blood burst from his open mouth, *plop*, and hit the carpet in one big, soggy drop. Henry felt the answering twitch of his own neck muscles, the jerk back of his own lowered head. "Lung," Cipriano said.

"What?"

"Must have touched the lung. That's when it comes up in bubbles like that. Don't worry. He's dead all right."

"Just as well it was you who did it," Henry said. It seemed an unusually long sentence. "I might have missed him."

"At that range? ... No."

"Missed the heart, I mean."

"It's nearer the middle of the body than most people think."

Henry straightened up, wiping the palms of his hands on the front of his jacket. Another inadvertent gesture, he wasn't sweating. If anything, he felt cold. The air conditioning had to be fully on. He was perfectly in control of himself, though. It was just that his reactions seemed oddly slowed. Breathe in, now. Breathe deep. Santi lay at his feet behind the sofa, not breathing at all.

One outflung, twisted hand was touching the leg of a small table. On the table was a framed photograph. Anita sitting on a bathing towel, Anita in a bikini. Henry stared at her. He hadn't seen that photograph before. The table, yes; the table had been there the night of the party. But not the photograph. Or if so, he'd missed it.

"Shut the door," Cipriano said.

Henry closed the door, feeling the self-locking device clicking over through the wood, under his hand; the door seemed sentient, living, after the sullen weight of Santi's corpse. When he turned back, he saw that Cipriano had moved over to the window and was looking down towards the office block; his face and shoulders, out of the direct rays of the overhead light, showed in near-silhouette.

"You were right, Henry. This is perfect. *Perfect*."

The shoulders were hunched, pulled a little forward, or was it a trick of the light? He didn't seem tense, otherwise. But what if he *was* tense? Anyone might be. It was funny, though, about that photograph. Henry turned his head, looking round the dimly-lit room.

"A real grandstand view. It couldn't be better."

"Cipriano," Henry said.

"Just five minutes to spare. Nice timing, too."

"Cipriano..."

"What's the matter?"

No need to reply. He had followed the direction of Henry's gaze and had seen it too. Over in the far, the shaded part of the huge room, away from the overhead lamp. He pushed his hands into his pockets and sauntered over to the polished table, sucking his teeth noisily. "Yes. I see. Expecting company, was he?" He took an Italian breadstick from the silver tray and bit at it experimentally. "Dinner with dear old dad, I shouldn't wonder." He moved round the table, took a bottle from the ice-bucket and patted it. "It's only just gone on ice. You get the picture...? Business first,

pleasure afterwards. Only there isn't going to be any afterwards. No problem."

"The table's laid for three," Henry said.

"*Claro.* Hernandez, too."

"Oh yes. Of course."

There were tall red candles in silver candlesticks. Cipriano took from his pocket a box of wax matches, struck one
and began to light the candles. "Someone's gone to a lot of
trouble, obviously. And it seems a pity to waste it altogether.
There. Isn't that delightful?" He shook out the match,
dropped it on the floor. "Come on, Henry. Try the *entre-
meses.* Have a stuffed olive."

The flames gained in brightness on top of the tall
sticks. Michael Faraday. The girl with saliva dribbling
down her chin, like melted wax. The whiteness of the
tablecloth, the muted glow of the silver; red and pallid
yellow of fresh-cut carnations. Impressions, memories,
random thoughts, and something wrong, something
wrong somewhere. Henry, striving to impose order on the
perplexed confusion in his brain, said,

"Flowers."

"Very nice, too," Cipriano said, biting again at the breadstick. "Colourful."

"Would he have flowers for *men*?"

The rhythm of the crunching stopped for a moment,
then continued. "You know more about gracious living
than I do, Henry. But it *must* be Martorell. Who else would
it be?"

"Yes," Henry said. "You're right."

"And whoever it is, it'll never happen. No need to
worry."

He was stretching out his hand towards the trimmed
salami when the sharp, brittle purr of the telephone stopped him dead. Henry's head came round again, this time
in an anxious jerk, his ears zeroing him in on the source
of the sound before his brain—still confused, still slow-

147

moving—had properly analysed it. Then with realisation came a sudden panic. "But, *Jesus—*"

"It's not that one, it's the other. The one in the bedroom, *caramba.* Don't you remember?" Cipriano, moving as unhurriedly as before, walked across the room to where the white telephone stood in its little private wall niche. He stood still for a moment, one hand on the receiver: "You're nervous, Henry," he said, and picked it up. *"Digame?"*

The voice at the other end was so loud that Henry, at three paces' distance, could hear it quite clearly. "Don Santiago...? We've just had word from Malaga. Your father's car is right on time. He'll be here in five minutes."

"Gracias," Cipriano said, and put down the receiver.

Now—perhaps because Henry's ears were still straining to listen—the silence abruptly struck. Nowhere in the room was there sound, or movement other than the dance of the candle flames. Empty of people, of sound, of music, the room seemed smaller than before, not larger, yet for a moment Henry felt lost in it as in a railway terminus, uncertain what to do, which way to turn.

"Five minutes," Cipriano said.

"Yes. I heard. What happens when Santi doesn't...?" He nodded towards the window. "...Show up?"

"He's always late," Cipriano said. "Nobody'll notice."

"The old man's bound to notice."

"Henry," Cipriano said. "You're nervous. And you talk too much."

"I just like to look ahead. That's all."

"All the looking ahead's been done already. From now on, all we do is follow the plan. And there's only one thing you have to worry about—when that 'plane leaves, you'd better be on it. Because for you, there'll be no second chances. For me, yes. But not for you, baby."

"I'll be on it all right," Henry said.

In fact it cost him an effort to wrench his thoughts

that far into the future. The airport, the take-off, the flight and England lay at an immeasurable distance from him, as once—lying in bed on the first night of term—had seemed the holidays; now, as then, his concern was uniquely with the present, a present coupled then with misery, now with fear. "But one day," he said, "I'll be back." As he had come to terms with the one, so would he now master the other. "One day soon."

"Yes," Cipriano said. "Maybe you will."

5

The Mercedes swung smoothly in to the side of the road
and came to a stop. The chauffeur got out, grey-uniformed,
impassive, and opened the back door with a flourish. Then
the other cars came by with glaring headlights, the two
black Fords of the Policia Armada followed closely by the
three Land Rovers of the Guardia Civil and the Buick with
the civil registration plate; the Buick turned in to park
neatly directly behind the Mercedes, while the others went
on to wheel sharp left, each in turn, and to stop in a
straggly file behind the office block. Headlamps flickered
off, motors cut; there were shouted orders in the darkness
and the staccato stamping of feet. "Anyone'd think,"
Martorell said, "we were politicians," and the man sitting
beside him—tall and very thin, his face the colour of the
chauffeur's uniform—snickered more in politeness than
amusement. He was reaching down, while he laughed, for
the heavy leather brief-case that lay on the Mercedes' buff-
carpeted floor, and held it in readiness across his lap.

The man from the passenger seat of the Buick was standing now beside the chauffeur, glancing with no great concern at the lighted office windows, then looking back at the
car as Martorell eased all eighteen stone of himself out on
to the pavement, straightening up to six foot three as he
nodded to the chauffeur's salute. Quite a target, (the police
lieutenant thought, as he walked quickly towards the main
door,) and quite a contrast to the other fellow now dis-
mounting. One tall and bulky, the other tall and cadaverous; and between them, about nine hundred million
pesetas. He stood by the door, easing his pistol-holster
forwards, as Martorell came up to it, mounting the steps

cumbrously, the famous heavy black cowlick of hair falling
across his forehead; inside, the white-collar boys stood in an
expectant group, one of them advancing, hand already extended. Hernandez was following close behind and the
man from the Buick, his right hand thrust deep into his
coat pocket, was at Hernandez' heels. The lieutenant—
like all police officers—hadn't much time for personal body-
guards; but if they had to exist, it was better if they knew
their job. This one did. From the moment the bulletproof
door of the Mercedes had been opened, the man from the
Buick had been right in place, screening his subjects from
the street behind—insofar as you *can* screen from fire a
shambling great bear and a bloody beanpole. It was just
as well, perhaps. The Civil Guard had been far too bloody
slow, as usual. But there was nothing, of course, he could
do about that; he had no jurisdiction over the Civis, and
anyway the C.O. of the detachment was a major. Here he
came now. A hard-faced bastard with a hairline moustache.
He came to attention, saluted.

"So far, so good, Major."

"I'm deploying my men around the building," the Major
said. "I suggest you use yours to cover the main entrance
here and the turning off the road." Though it'll all be a
waste of time, his attitude suggested. We've had wild goose
chases with you bloody cops before.

"Those were my instructions, Major. They should be in
position by now."

"Good," the Major said. "That's okay, then."

They stood each of them now in the at ease position,
hands folded behind their backs, staring at each other.
Neither knew what to say next. Henry, peering down at
them from high aloft and sensing their frustration, had to
resist a peculiar temptation to throw open the window and
to bawl out at them at the top of his voice. *Aquí, cabrónes!*
...Anything to break the deadlock. Instead he turned back
towards the quietly-lit penthouse room, where Cipriano sat

151

sprawled in one of Santi's armchairs leafing through *Die Erotik in der Kunst* and looking at the dirty pictures. He couldn't read the text because it was in German; Cipriano couldn't read German. Nor could Santi, if it came to that. He couldn't before, and he certainly couldn't now, lying on his back behind the sofa. Henry could still feel the shout bottled up, as it were, at the base of his throat; it was the quietness, the silence. It made you want to explode in it like a bomb.

"Ramona was wrong," he said. "They both came in the same car. They've gone in."

Cipriano flipped the book shut, put it down on the arm of the chair. "And the fuzz?"

"They've sort of spread out. All round the office."

"Yes. They know something's up. So they've changed the plan. They probably thought it'd make things easier for the escort if they travelled together. A good sign, that is."

"Why?"

"Shows they expected trouble on the road. They know something's up all right, but they can't have much of a clue as to what."

He raised his hands ceilingwards, stretched himself; then stood up and walked over to the window. He peered down, as had Henry, from behind the folds of the blue velvet curtain.

"So Ramona hasn't ... ?"

"It looks as though she hasn't," Cipriano said. And, as an afterthought,

"From now on, Henry, walk. Don't run."

"*Look* ... They're in the office."

"So I see. Try and keep your voice down, will you? No one's likely to hear us, but still ... there's no need to shout."

"I wasn't shouting," Henry said.

"All right. Just cool it."

He took from his inside pocket the 16X sniperscope he had decided to use in preference to the field-glasses; more compromising, but a great deal less bulky. Open-mouthed in concentration, he focused the screw lenses on the office window. "It looks nice," he said. "Very nice. The old man's right there at the desk, where we thought he'd sit. And Hernandez ... He's going to sit down opposite him. There. It looks very good." He swung the little telescope further round. The Civil Guard major was walking up and down the road outside the office with a slow, pensive strut; the police lieutenant had disappeared, probably to have a quiet drag somewhere round the corner. Cipriano searched the shadows behind the building, but couldn't spot him.

"Get ready," he said.

The direct line ran to the telephone in the bedroom; on the night table, beside the bed. You couldn't see the office from there. So Henry, standing at the head of the bed, would get the signal from Cipriano at the window. Then Henry would lift the telephone, press the call button and that would be that.

But not just yet. There were papers in Hernandez' brief-case, papers for signature, papers that in a minute, or five minutes, or ten, would be spread out on the desk. The papers had to go as well. That was important. All this Ramona had explained; all this Henry knew. He hadn't forgotten it. But he didn't move. Couldn't. It was true; he was getting nervous. It was the silence, mostly. And the long file of police vehicles, parked outside. Walk, Henry. Don't run. He'd remember.

"Get ready," Cipriano said again. "Go and stand by the 'phone. Don't even touch the bugger, though, till I tell you."

"God, we've been through all this—"

"*Leche*, don't argue. Just do it."

—his voice rising several tones above its normal timbre, gritty with contained impatience. Henry turned and walked towards the bedroom door, which stood wide open, waiting for him; through it he could see the turned-down double

153

bed with its crimson counterpane, the night table with its array of sun-lotion bottles, with its blinker alarm clock, with its telephone; the telephone also waiting for him, black plastic snugly coiled in the cradle, white-circled hood of the dialling key, harmless, familiar, deadly, cobra-head of technology reared to strike. His feet padded softly across the thick bedroom carpet; red counterpane, turned-down sheets, something wrong, something wrong, wrong, *wrong*, a sensation now so powerful that he stopped. The door bell rang. He looked back at Cipriano; who stood at the window, motionless, head twisted over one lowered shoulder. For twenty seconds, neither of them moved.

Then the door bell rang again. It rang with a determined, near-manic insistence, stopped unexpectedly. From behind the door a voice, barely audible, called,

"...*Santi?*"

and Cipriano turned away at last from the window, a slow, dragging movement reluctant as a sigh, slipping the revolver from its shoulder holster. "Don't let her in," Henry said, urgently. And Cipriano, not looking at him,

"We have to. We can't let her go away."

"It's *Anita*."

"Don't worry. You stay where you are, in the bedroom. I'll look after it."

"But not that way again."

Cipriano, one hand on the release spring of the door lock, shook his head; no longer impatient, gently comprehending. "She *knows* us, Henry. We haven't any choice. Leave it all to me." The door swinging open. "Hullo," he said.

"Oh..." Anita's voice, small, uncertain. "I thought—"

"Santi'll be back in a moment. Come on in."

The door, opening wider. Cipriano's hand behind the panel, the snub revolver-barrel projecting from the brown bent fingers. *Just do it. It's no good thinking, talking. Don't argue. Just do it.* And of course it would be easy; easier

154

than the other. She'd take two or three paces into the room and the muzzle of the revolver would circle from behind the door and rise to touch the nape of her neck and jerk once; and then Cipriano would close the door again. He was right, after all. She knew them both. She had seen Henry now, Henry coming quickly forwards from the bedroom, and had stopped, her huge gazelle-eyes huger with surprise. "Henry, what on earth..." The revolver was coming up behind her; Henry's contorted face would be the last thing those big wide eyes would see. He flung his whole weight at her behind his stiffened right arm, thrusting her with all his strength back against Cipriano, who let out a little agonised puppy-like *woof* as her elbow jerked to impact against his stomach. Caught off-balance on high heels, she sprawled absurdly on the carpet, arms and legs out at all angles, while Henry's right hand on Cipriano's wrist forced the revolver upwards and away. "Not *that* way, not *that* way." They struggled uncertainly and with a curious ineptitude, bumping into one another like straphanging passengers jostled in a crowded tube train. Then Anita screamed. She'd seen Santi, of course.

"Mierda, kill the bitch."

It was a beautiful, full-blooded Spanish scream, starting off with a whirr in the throat like the sound of a startled partridge and then rising like a rocket; and for a moment, equally appalled, the two men broke off their bewildered combat by the door to stare at her. Then Cipriano, in sudden fury, broke free and slashed at Henry's head with the barrel of the revolver, landing a glancing blow that furrowed blood across one temple and sent Henry cannoning back against the wall. The rebound took him full tilt into Cipriano's chest; Cipriano staggered and they fell to the floor together, Henry uppermost, wrestling once again for possession of the revolver. Almost at once, it went off; the photograph frame on the side table exploded in a hurtle of fragmented glass and leaped into the air to land and

155

skitter face upwards across the floor; Anita, in her Galerias Preciados bikini, went on laughing hopefully up towards the ceiling, a brown hole punched in her taut-muscled belly, while the other Anita, also on the floor, continued to do her best to scream the place down. "Shut up," Henry shouted despairingly. "Shut *up*, you silly bitch." She took no notice.

"Henry." Cipriano's face was some three inches from his own, its lips curled back. They seemed now to be immoveably embraced, like Rodin's lovers. "Let go of me."

"You'll kill her, if I do."

"If you don't, I'll kill you both."

There was little doubt but that he meant it. Henry hesitated. But then suddenly, weirdly, Anita was on top of them, her fists pummelling a frantic tattoo on Henry's back. "Stop it, stop it *both* of you, what's going *on*?" Cipriano, convulsed with rage again at this ridiculous intervention, tore his wrist free and aimed a savage blow at Henry's head with the revolver; his fingers, partially numbed, lost their grip and it scuttered, spinning, across the floor. They started to roll over and over on the carpet, all three of them, clawing at each other's clothes as though engaged in some interesting species of sexual encounter, thrusting out a hand from time to time in search of leverage then bringing it back, invariably empty, to pummel in desperation at each other's back or ribs, as variously presented. Anita, the first to detach herself, got to her feet and tried the door; but it had closed and the impact of its closing had shot the safety lock and she couldn't get the hang of it. She tore at the sliding catch with her fingers, making little whimpering noises under her breath, while Henry and Cipriano grunted and bumped against her ankles. She was much too frightened to observe the ineffectiveness of the combatants; men were maniacs, impervious to reason; she was very scared. But the bedroom door, she now saw, was open. She scampered through it, the

156

sound of muffled imprecations and furious thumpings following her. The bedroom door had a lock, too, and a key. She turned it. Now at least she could hide. In the wardrobe. Under the bed. Anywhere.

As she turned the key, ironically, the battle halted, for no other reason than temporary exhaustion. It had lasted for some ninety seconds, no more than that; Henry was bleeding from the cut on his temple and there was an answering red trickle from Cipriano's nose, but the damage mutually inflicted was negligible, really. It was just that neither of them was in training for this sort of thing. They knelt, gasping for breath, just out of arm's reach of one another. "...*Mira, somos locos. Pero locos.*"

"We can't kill her," Henry said. "That's all there is to it." He wiped blood from his cheek with the back of hand, stared at it in bemusement. "God, I'm bleeding."

"She'll talk."

"All right, so she'll talk. And Ramona'll talk. Everyone'll bloody well talk, sooner or later. Doesn't mean we'll have to ... *kill* everyone ... do we?" He had more to say, but no breath left with which to say it. "We can get away. We'll have time. We'll lock her up in there..."

He looked round, at the open bedroom door that wasn't open any more. "Hey," he said stupidly.

He got to his feet, shambled over to the door, bent double, started to tug at the handle. "Anita...? Anita...?" No reply. "She's locked it," he said, turning back towards Cipriano. Cipriano had found the revolver again and had picked it up and was pointing it more or less in Henry's direction. A sharp, painful blossom of white flowered from the levelled barrel; the door jumped and splintered against the palms of his hands. "Wait!" Henry shouted, *"Wait!"* —jerking away from the door, and just in time; Cipriano wasn't a very good shot, but the second shot would have taken him chest-high if he hadn't jumped clear. Anita, somewhere behind the door, was screaming again. His

157

frantic side-step had taken him to the wall panel where the electric-light tumble switches projected in a neat white plastic row; the revolver barrel was moving after him, catching him up, and he swept his hand desperately over the panel in the vague hope of turning out all the lights and diving into darkness. In fact, and on the instant, the opposite happened; the lights didn't go out, but turned instead into shifting multi-coloured streams in which Cipriano and the revolver and the white flame of the third shot dissolved like snowflakes and were lost. That bullet came the nearest of the three, but didn't hit him, either. He stood stock-still, rivetted in astonishment, while from hidden overhead amplifiers the ghosts of long-haired guitarists began to raise a plaintively hideous cacophony. Unbelievable, and yet familiar; he'd seen this before, the night of Santi's party. He'd switched on Santi's private party Happening.

Cipriano, who hadn't seen it before, was lost not only to Henry but indeed to himself in the centre of the floor, was swept away in a flowing river of bright colour; moving to his left in utter bewilderment, he banged into a table and knocked it over. A glass ash tray shivered to extinction on the floor, a thousand facets of crimson light winking and blinking out. From that tiny explosion of colour, great dahlias of yellow flame petalled out around him, turning to paler snowballs of floating fire; he raised the pistol and fired again, the recoil jarring his wrist, the bark of the leaping gases lost in the furious jumping thrumming of guitars and saxes, while a hoarse voice began to bawl incomprehensible instructions at him. He himself was shouting, but meaninglessly, his lips framing the words—*Turn it off, turn it off!*—but he couldn't hear the sound of his own voice; he tugged wildly at the trigger and the revolver vibrated again, he heard *that*, and then, in the small of his back—mysteriously—and against his screwed-up eyes, another explosion, this time of a bright, a glaring blue, shading off into purple, and from its white-hot centre a coldness spread, catching at his knees, his elbows, so that the weight of the revolver pendulumed his arm downwards and, following its slow, irresistible swing, the vividly-patterned carpet lurched up at him. *Doncha*, the voices bellowed ... *step on ma blue suede shoes* ... No feeling, no pain when the pattern hit him; only the sudden careering of mad blue stars across the evening sky, the billowing swell of orange clouds. A whiteness, a coldness. His right knee, straightening. His fingers, stiff, frozen. The music dimming, becoming a part of that coldness. Turn off, turn off. The current fast fading. His mind had had no time to get to grips with this new, this unexpected problem, and now the power wasn't getting through. He would never solve it. Probably, he thought, there's no answer to this one, anyway. And never will be.

Henry stood with one hand on the switch panel, the other holding the Luger, still levelled. The lights were now back to normal, but the shadows still seemed to dance and throb. Cipriano, agonised on the floor beside the upturned table, Cipriano too seems to move. But doesn't. The Luger is a terrifying weapon, at close range. The bullet's impact is so tremendous that its shock shatters the nerve-endings, kills the pain; it spins you backwards like a blow from a heavy-weight boxer, and if it touches a vital centre you're dead before you can kick. Cipriano's spine had been split like a twig. Henry stared at him, unmoving; only the tiny muscles at the corners of his eyes twitched. Again he was aware of that taste at the back of his throat, brassy, like vomit. Had he really *meant* to do it...? He wasn't sure. He, too, needed time. He stood with one hand on the switch panel, the other holding the Luger, while the seconds moved gently past and nothing happened.

But the silence was worst of all. Silence; that was all Nothing.

there was. There was nothing left now to listen to. Anita stood behind the door, her head drooping on its slender neck. Her hand was on the doorkey; she stared at it, but didn't dare turn it. Her hair had collapsed from its carefully-arranged ringlets down over her eyes; her velvet dress was torn open from neck to waist. Of course there was the window. She could always open the window. And scream.

Or hide. She could hide under the bed. Or in the wardrobe. But suppose they were dead, both of them? And if they weren't, they'd find her in any case. It'd be easy. There was only the bed, the wardrobe, the bathroom ... The bathroom? Another locked door, at least, to be broken down. And perhaps another window. A fire escape? She had to call for help. Suppose there was...

Her head was lifted now, was stiffened with hope. Beside her was the bed and the night table; and on the night table, the telephone, gleaming and black on its cradle. There it was all the time; the answer to her problem, if she was quick. "Oh yes," she said out loud.

She ran towards it.

When she lifted the 'phone and pressed the call button, this then is how it was: — Martorell seated at the desk, the tips of his fingers pressed together lightly, frowning at the memory of some distant perplexity; Hernandez who sat directly opposite him with his brief-case, open, on his knees and the Sotomayor schedules in his right hand, his eyes turned downwards towards them in search of a relevant paragraph; the man in grey, who stood by the open door gazing down the empty corridor ... These three were killed at once, were seized and squeezed, as it were gently, by the trigger-finger of the detonation; it held them for a second, no longer, collapsed their lungs and dropped them at once, sprawled like puppets, on the floor. Sparks glowed for a few instants on the sleeve and lapels of Martorell's faultlessly-tailored suit, then went out; Hernandez' suit, on the other hand, and shirt, were ripped to tatters by the explosion which left the shocking whiteness of his naked chest exposed though quite unmarked; while the door, blasted, though open, off its hinges, drove a nine-inch-long splinter of itself through the back of the bodyguard's neck and into his brain. The Civil Guard patrolling just outside the window was caught in a razor-edged hail of flying glass and was tossed to the ground, a meaningless pattern of dark bloodstains growing around the slashes in his olive-green uniform, while his partner, a pace or two to the right and a fraction to the rear, was blown fifteen feet down the road like a paper bag caught in a funnelled gust of wind and stayed where he fell, unconscious, with a fractured skull. It was he, though, who survived. The police lieutenant, in the shelter of the wall, felt the air rock and heave about him a split second before the doomsday crack of the explosion pressed at his eardrums and dust and glass and metal slivers sprayed over the pavement; he sank to his knees, clutching at his head, then got back to his feet and lurched towards what remained of the office door in a staggering run. He was in time to see the last of the heavy plaster flakes settling on the body of the man in the grey suit and, through the ravaged door and blackened brickwork, the sharp metallic glow of the magnesium flame. There were shouts, cries, the crunch on gravel of heavy booted feet. He stood motionless, fingers splayed against the hot wall, holding himself upright, knowing only that there was nothing he could do. He had seen magnesium flares before.

Hands clutched at his waist, at his shoulders. "Are you all right, Teniente?"

"Yes," he said. "I'm all right." He was surprised to hear his own voice firm and resonant.

"What about . . . ?"

161

Them. Yes. Nothing to be done.

"They're dead," he said. "Cordon off the building. And send for the fire brigade. That's all we can do."

"You did it," Henry said. "Christ. *You* did it."

"Did what?"

He had broken in the bedroom door while the after-echoes of the explosion were still dying, while the heavy glass chandelier above the bed still quivered from the vibration. And Anita, the telephone in her hand, had stared at him from the head of the bed, white-faced, expressionless, yet somehow accusingly. Then he had turned and gone to the penthouse window, to look down at the clear white light of the flames boxed in the office window, at the dark shapes that shouted, that ran to and fro, aimlessly, pointlessly, like insects. No mountain there below; no majestic plume of smoke, no mushroom billow; just a small house on fire, running men, screams. He went back to the bedroom, not quite believing it.

"Are you all right?"

"Yes," Anita said. "I'm all right," and started to laugh. She lay down to laugh, burying her face in the pillow. Her shoulders shook. The receiver was still clutched, though loosely, in her hand; after a while, Henry went across to take it from her and to set it carefully down once again in its cradle. He thought, *it worked. That much at least we know. This time it worked.*

"Anita. Listen. We've got to go."

She was crying now, rather than laughing. She took no notice of him at all; it was as though she hadn't heard him. He realised he was still carrying the Luger in his right hand. He placed it—again carefully—on the table beside the telephone, then took her shoulders in both hands and shook her. She didn't resist and didn't respond. It was like shaking a doll. A doll that wailed. He stopped and watched her for a few moments, his hands thrust deep into his pockets; then went back to the other room and looked once more out the window. The flames were brighter now, were break ing out of the box of window-frames, lighting up the length of the street beneath. He didn't know what to do.

Get out, that was obvious. But how...? Not in the car. That wasn't possible. Cipriano was dead. Henry couldn't drive. Anita, though, Anita could maybe drive. But even if she could, why should she? She couldn't be trusted. It was all her fault, Cipriano being dead, but she wouldn't see it that way. The flames pouring now through the gap-toothed holes of what had once been windows, burning higher and higher. A car came up the road, skidding to a halt. People jumped out. No, it was hopeless. Better to run for it, to cut down to the Malaga road and thumb a lift. But he'd never get there in time. Not to the airport. "Oh God," Henry said. Tears of frustration rolled down his cheeks.

He went back to the bedroom.

"Anita ... Can you drive?"

She was no longer audibly crying, but still didn't reply. "I've got a car down there. But I can't drive. Can you?" After a long pause,

"...No," she said.

He wasn't sure if he believed her. But there seemed no point in arguing. Go or stay...? The effort of decision was too great. He sat down at her feet, on the end of the bed, seeing, as he sat, that one of his shoelaces had come untied, probably in the struggle with Cipriano; he stooped to re-fasten it; a neat, symmetric bow. It was strange, how tired he felt. He closed his eyes and let time wash over him; a shimmering and iridescent veil. She could drive or she couldn't drive. It wasn't worth arguing.

Behind his eyelids the explosion happened again, this time soundlessly, its colour a delicate green; the pillar rose like a column of water and turned into a young tree, a springtime eruption, sunlight glittering on its freshborn leaves. The water ran down to form a pool in its shadow; there was water beneath it, a lake, a plank bridge, and on the bridge he stood, the wood trembling distantly under his feet. The water was calm and colourless, except near the banks where the reeds and bulrushes tinged it with an echo of beechen green and with touches of yellow. A dabchick then, scuttering across the flawless surface of Henry's mind, splashing water from its flying wingtips; and then he saw again the tree, great green explosion, erected against the sky. He could reach out and touch with his fingers the soft roughness of the bark, feel the underlying strength and rigidity. And its silence; above all, its silence. The leaves moving in the sunlight, but making no sound; that's what one misses in Spain, Henry thought, the rustle of trees in the wind. Here there's the sun, fire; fire burns, roars, crackles. He opened his eyes.

"Why aren't there any damned clocks in this place?"

Anita, too, was now sitting up on the bed, watching him. Still not replying, but then, she might well not know the answer to that particular question. Maybe Santi simply hadn't liked clocks. Not everyone cares to be reminded of time, of the great hallucination. How old had he been, standing on that bridge...? Five? Seven? There was no way of remembering. Henry looked at his wrist-watch and saw that it was segmented, like a bisected orange; there was a pattern there and nothing but a pattern. "It wasn't me who killed him, you know. It was Cipriano."

This time she replied. "Cipriano?" ... If you called that a reply.

"The other one. He wanted to kill you, too. I had to stop him."

"But why?"

She had moved a little closer, was stooped towards him; one hand edged out on the mattress, as though about to touch him. But not touching him. Not yet. "What was that awful ... bang?"

Not a flower. A tree. Moving in the wind, but silently. "There was a bomb," Henry said, "in the office. We put it there. Cipriano and me."

"Then it was ... in the office? Not his *father*?"

"Yes. And there was another man. I forget his name. He wanted to kill you, though, you realise that?"

"You stopped him."

"I shot him. I think he's dead."

"Yes." She lifted her hand from the bed to dab at loose, fallen tendrils of black hair. "Henry, can we go now?"

He still hadn't made up his mind. "No. Not yet."

"I don't like it up here."

But he had to decide something. He could see *that*. "You don't understand. They were trying to make a fool of me, I'm sure of that. Yes, they had it all worked out. I was never meant to get away at all ... I can see that now. He was going to kill me. Me and you. Both. Then they could have put the blame on me. So it's no good running—that's what he meant, that about *even if you run*—and it was all lies about that aeroplane. That's what I was supposed to do—run away. And then get caught. No. No, we're staying here."

"But how long?"

"I don't know how long."

No clocks. There weren't any clocks. Henry got up and went through to the sitting-room, but there weren't any clocks there, either. There was Santi's body and Cipriano's body; yes, Cipriano was dead all right. He lay, face upwards, very near the place where the girl with the hole in her dress had lain; he too, had a hole in his dress, black-stained and wet. They had all come to Henry's party, to the *real* party, had all been made a part of his wild illusion; the candles still burnt there on the table; nothing made any sense. They were the true innocents; he the swinger, he the destroying angel. "Santi, he was just in the way. He wasn't even meant to be here."

"But he *lives* here."

"I know that. We know that. Yes, and what about you?"

"Me?"

"Yes, you. What brought *you* here?"

"He invited me to dinner. To meet—"

"Dinner, oh yes. To dinner."

The candles burning, tall and phallic. The table lay overturned beside Cipriano's body; the magazines that had stood on it were strewn over the carpet, one of them spattered with dark spots of blood. Henry picked it up. "Dinner. I know all about *that*, too." It wasn't just his hands. His whole body was trembling; silently, silently. The glossy pages were shaken open in his fingers. "What about this, then? All this ... dirty filth ...?" Naked man and naked woman; his hands resting on her hips, as at the opening figure of a formal dance. Staring at each other's bodies with a fixed, a mindless intensity. On the opposite page, the same two bodies writhed, motionless, on a stripped-down bed; the girl's mouth wide open, her eyes glittering, devoid of sight, in the glare of the cameraman's Klieg lamp. "That's how it ends up, isn't it? That's how *you'd* have ended up. You and him. As if you didn't know it. It's filthy, filthy."

A red smear had appeared on the edge of his knuckles. She stared at the blood, not at the picture, her lips drawn back in disgusted fascination: "It wasn't like that at all. I was going to meet his father. We were—"

"He never showed you pictures like that?" Henry hurled the magazine across the room, so violently that she stepped quickly backwards. "Waiting for you here, wasn't he? That's what spoiled it all. You spoiled the whole bloody thing, between the two of you. Just because you—"

"Oh shut up, *shut up, SHUT UP.*"

And she clapped her hand hard over her own mouth. No, she thought; I won't scream, I won't go to pieces again. I'm sane and he's mad ... or something ... and sane has to be better. Sane gives me maybe some kind of a chance. If I can hold on to it. It was the other one, after all, who tried to kill me. Not Henry. He said so. Henry wouldn't kill me. *Henry...?* Not ever...

The shadows of the candle flames, moving on the wall, and behind them other, paler shadows; the echoes of the flames below where the office block was burning now like matchwood. While Henry had become once more, apparently, calm, his thin face emptied of passion, indeed of emotion. He turned towards the windows and, reaching up for the heavy woven cord, pulled the curtains; they ran across with a dry reptilian rattle, settled their folds and were still. He crossed the room without looking at her again and sat down at the dining-table.

"All this wine and silver and stuff. All laid out for you, like that bed in there. All right. Come on. It's a pity to waste it. Come on, then. Sit down."

He waved her to the chair directly opposite him. She walked nervously past Santi's slowly-stiffening body and sat down. "There," Henry said. "That's nice." His hands, she noticed, now weren't trembling at all; the blood had dried in a fine, unbroken thread across his right knuckles. "I know how it's done, you see—this romantic stuff. What else...? Ah, yes." He nodded to himself. "Of course. Sweet music. I knew there was something."

He went to the radiogram behind Anita's chair and turned it on. The ceiling amplifiers crackled as they took up the relay, whined loudly as he fiddled with the selector knob; then there it was. Sweet and stereophonic. Violins. A symphony orchestra, by the sound of it; Schubert or Mendelssohn. Anita's eyes were focussed on the table in front of her, where silver gleamed warmly and also steel; the carving-knife and fork, beside the chafing-dish. Polished steel, honed to a beautiful edge. "Very nice," Henry said, sitting down opposite her again. "Now we can eat."

"I'm not hungry," Anita said.

The fire-hoses were turned upwards now to their highest angle of elevation, spraying the water from above instead of directing their questing jets to the centre of the blaze; the fireman's admission of defeat. The police lieutenant stood, soaked to the skin, at the periphery; his eyes were aching badly, the skin of his face was blistered, and he took off his gloves to press the dry lids with his fingertips. His feet, like those of the Civil Guard major beside him, were braced apart as though ready to meet an assault; and indeed tomorrow, metaphorically, the wall would fall on them, and they both knew it. "We were informed too late," the major said, "to take the proper precautions. That's the line we have to take. Don't you agree?"

"Nothing was thrown. That's for sure."

"A time mechanism, almost certainly."

"That's not possible, either. We had time to get in the mikes—they'd have picked up the sound."

"That's all right if they believe it. Who tested the room?"

"Ibor."

"He's in trouble. There was something there all right— no doubt about *that*."

"We're all in trouble," the lieutenant said.

"We didn't have time to take the proper precautions. That's the only line for us to take, believe you me."

One of the fire-hoses sputtered and stopped, water trickling gently from its raised nozzle. The supply was failing; that, too, was inevitable. The firemen commenced to coil it, while the other hose went on, its spray at half-speed swinging to and fro, to and fro, to faintly hypnotic effect. The major and the lieutenant watched it, unmoving.

"Who's to be notified?"

"The B.D. boys will be here in fifteen minutes." The major hadn't heard the question properly, or hadn't understood. "We'll know a bit more about it then."

"I meant, who do we have to notify? ... Relatives?"

"First of all we have to find out for sure who's dead."

"Martorell. And Hernandez. No doubt about that."

"And that bodyguard feller. One of my men has probably copped it, if it comes to that." The major put his little finger in his ear and wiggled it, confirming the other's suspicions. "Murdering sods," he added.

"There's the son. Martorell's son. He's supposed to be around here somewhere."

"If he wasn't in there as well."

"Yes," the captain said, and sighed. "We'll wait for the Bomb Disposal crowd, then. Always better to check."

The knife raised high in the air, his hand balled round the hilt; lying on the carpet, arms outstretched, knees lifted, she screamed at him, "Don't, *Doooooooon't!*" not knowing her own voice because in the scream was neither fear nor pain nor any other known sensation; it was the vapid, meaningless cry of a slaughtered pig as the blade passes through its throat, a single sound stretched to infinity as the sharp steel circled and plunged. His body, as she saw, was stiffened, made tense by fury; the knife came down again and again, opening in the plump seat of the sofa a gaping black triangle through which a tongue of red foam rubber poked obscenely. *Filth*, the knife said, slashing, slashing; *filth, filth, filth*; Henry's breath puffing now through his teeth as his rigid forearm rose and fell. The cushioned sofa-back, mutilated, torn, metal there twanging softly as the knife-point jarred against a spring; Anita closed her eyes, but could still hear the sound of his panting through a red and black curtain, the thump and rip of the blows.

He had hurt her, taking the knife from her. There was pain where he had forced back her wrist, twisted her shoulder; pain where, in falling, her hip had struck the floor; and her dress now open to the waist, black velvet split at the seams and ruined. The rhythm of the knife-thrusts slackened and stopped. The sound of his breathing continued, heavy, the rasp of a badly-worn file. She opened her eyes.

He knelt beside her, looking down at her. His right hand was empty; he held it out, fingers extended, towards her bare shoulder without touching it; and his rage, so far as she could tell, was gone with the knife, gone as suddenly as it had come. He was mad, of course he was mad. But she had been stupid. The knife—what could she have done with it? She hadn't meant to attack him with it. She'd just wanted to defend herself. To have at least the chance of . . .

"Why?" Henry said. There was no anger in his voice. He seemed simply perplexed.

"I know. It was stupid."

"You made me lose my temper."

"I wasn't going to hurt you."

"I didn't mean to hurt you, either. I'm not like that, really. I try to be . . . you know. Calm."

Dark tendrils of her hair were spread on the red carpet, framing the upturned oval of her face. He moved his hand and, at last, touched her; he touched her hair, lifting one ringlet, smoothing it out. "*Did* I hurt you?"

"Not really. Just when I fell."

"It wasn't my fault. You tripped. You lost a shoe."

"I don't remember."

"Can you get up?"

It was true. She had lost a shoe. She kicked the other one off and got to her feet, Henry's hand at her elbow steadied her with gentlemanly compassion. She tried to pull her dress into place, but the shoulder-straps had gone completely; it was all right, though. She wasn't really hurt. She sat down on the savaged sofa and closed her eyes. "Why did you . . . ?"

"What?"

"It doesn't matter."

"I told you. I lost my temper."

"That's what you wanted to do to *me*. You did it to the sofa, instead."

"No," Henry said. His voice sounded placid, reasonable. "I don't want to hurt you. I couldn't." And after a pause, *"You're* not really like that, either."

"Like what?"

"With your dress all . . ."

He stopped and, when she opened her eyes, was standing with his back towards her. "You shouldn't have come here."

"No," Anita said. It was only her bruised hip that hurt her now; holding the dress together across her breasts, she massaged it with her free hand. She shouldn't have come; that was true, too. "Look, I don't know if I would or wouldn't have. That's the truth."

"Wouldn't have what?"

"Have gone to bed with him. Since that's what seems to be worrying you."

"No, I don't suppose you would have."

"Well, if you—" Checking herself abruptly. "But his father was coming to dinner. It just wouldn't have arisen."

"No? Not afterwards?"

"I told you. I just don't *know*." It was incredible, his capacity—even in these circumstances—to provoke these familiar spasms of near-maternal irritation. He still stood with his back to the sofa, not even looking at her. "Haven't you got other things to worry about, for God's sake?"

"What other things?"

"You've got to get out of here, haven't you? The police'll be coming."

"Better to stay where we are," Henry said. His voice

was still placidly reasonable, holding indeed a tone of finality. "But we *can't* do that," she said.

"They won't come up here. Why should they?"

"Because they'll wonder what's happened to..." For some reason, she couldn't say the name. He might have heard her, lying there behind the sofa. "They'll miss him. They're bound to."

"They've no reason to suppose he's here. He'd have gone down, wouldn't he?—after hearing a bang like that. They may even think he was in the office when it happened. And in that case—"

"But why can't we go to your room? Or to mine? It'd be much safer."

Henry didn't reply. And almost at once, from its niche in the corner of the room, the telephone began to buzz discreetly. Anita turned her head with a jerk. The sound had frightened her.

"Let it ring," Henry said.

Cipriano hadn't liked the English.

Why not?

But if it came to that, why should he? Henry's question had had no real significance, anyway. Merely idle Spanish chitchat, occupying an idle Spanish lunch-hour. "They take an interest in things. They won't leave things alone."

"I thought you were in favour of change yourself."

"Change is what happens if you *do* leave things alone. Change is the natural order. But the English—they're conservative. They're in favour of conservation. They think Spaniards are a fascinating species of wild life that ought to be carefully protected. Along with flamenco, bullfights and all the rest of it. Before long they'll be shutting us up in little enclaves—typical Spanish villages full of typical Spanish peasants, all having typical Spanish children and being picturesquely ravaged with seventeen different kinds of typical Spanish pox. All just the way Cervantes saw it. And Goya. The *real* Spain. It'll all go the way of Torremolinos if the English don't step in and protect it, because the Spaniards can't be trusted. No, I don't like the English. Not at all."

A great talker, Cipriano.

"But *can* the Spaniards be trusted?"

"That's like asking, can life be trusted? Of course it can't. But then it's our country. There's no real choice."

The pavement bar at Los Boliches; the frustrated roaring of bottle-necked lorries; far in the distance, the mountain peak. And opposite them, the church; a new church, a modern church, on its near wall a futuristically-designed sun, its rays cheerfully outspread like the figures on an oval clock face. "The English are human, too," Henry said. "You make them sound like God."

"I don't like God much, either," Cipriano had said.

Now—having no choice—he lay on his back, his shirt bunched under his broad shoulders, one knee a little raised, as though he were absorbing the rays of that unasked-for sun on a beach of red carpet, while behind him at last the telephone stopped ringing. He had been in life perhaps—as the police captain had said—a murdering sod; in death he seemed much less and quite certainly more, so that one could hardly say whether to that prostrate shape on the floor something had been added or subtracted. The voice, now silent, spoke on; but there would be no more idle chitchat in street bars or in tall white houses behind Malaga, no serious philosophical discussion ever over a bottle of wine, and Henry, looking at Cipriano and hearing his voice again, felt once more the pity of it. There should have been time for all that, but there hadn't been.

He still didn't much like the English. you could see that he didn't. As to what he now thought of God, there was no way of telling.

* * *

"I never thought you were *political*. You never said anything."

"It's not politics, exactly."

"But killing people. *You*. It's just unbelievable."

"It just happens to be me, that's all. It's me at one end, the way it just happened to be Santi on the other. We didn't have a choice—either of us."

"I don't understand," Anita said.

"Then don't ask questions."

"But if you want me to help—"

"I don't want you to help."

"Then why won't you let me *go*? I haven't done anything."

"I can't," Henry said. "You have to stay here."

"But I wouldn't tell anybody. Honest, I wouldn't. I mean, I don't have to. They're bound to catch you, anyway."

"Yes. I know they will."

"Henry, *please* let me go."

"You have to stay here. You haven't any choice. Any more than I have, or any of us. They'll catch us all right, even if we run."

"*Ay Dios. Ay Dios.*"

They were talking, for no special reason, in very low voices, the long exchange seeming to be of thoughts as much as of words or instead of words, though the sound of their low voices of course was there, their alternate sentences rattling against each other like the swords of fencers, flourished and disengaged. Now, speechless, they stared at each other, eye taking over from tongue the hopeless task of intercommunication. They sat apart, six feet between them, Anita on the sofa, Henry in an armchair, yet each felt the other close, as at grappling distance; they were linked by a strange sense of intimacy, physical yet not physical, as were, perhaps, Santi and Cipriano, united on the floor in death. The room was quiet, save for the faint moaning hum of the radiogram. On the dining-table, the candles had burned low.

"It's like being on top of a mountain," Henry said. "You and me."

"I've never been on top of a mountain."

"The thing about it is, all ways are down."

"But you *have* to go down. You can't stay stuck on top of a mountain for ever."

"I'm wondering about that," Henry said.

She didn't know what he meant but it was, in any case, just one meaningless remark among many. "Henry, are there ... others?"

"Other what?"

"Apart from you and *that* one. Cipriano."

"Oh yes. There must be. Hundreds of others."

"But ... anyone who can help you?"

"No," Henry said. "No one who can help. Nobody at all."

6

Thank God, was Bellido's reaction when the news came through. *It's over. We needn't go on.*

But following on that moment of relief, a wave of despondency; so much effort, so much pain, and all for nothing. It had happened. He had failed to avert it. There was no one to blame but himself. If, perhaps, he had been harder on himself, had seen his task as being something other than a thoroughly disagreeable necessity, or perhaps had been more persuasive, more sympathetic, more conciliatory ... *Perhaps; if only.* Now it was too late. Of course it had all happened before, but that didn't make things any better.

Back in the interrogation room, he took his jacket from the chair and slipped it on. He took his pencil and his empty black official notebook from the table, slipped them into his pocket. The prisoner lay motionless on the table, slitted pupils staring at the ceiling from the bloodless mask of her face, seeing nothing, feeling nothing, saying nothing. Above all, saying nothing. Saying nothing still. Bellido looked down at her, then reached over to lay his hot, dry palm once more across the back of her hand.

"It's over," he said. "Your people got him."

He thought that his fingers detected a tiny tremor.

"*Está bien.* You didn't talk. You were brave. Martorell could have gone back to Madrid. But no—he was brave, too. So now he's dead. So much bloody bravery. So much stupidity."

The tremor could have been of understanding, or of something else. The upturned, waxen face gave nothing away. He moved his fingers down to her pulse. There was nothing there, either.

"You did well, *mujer*. You did very well. But we'll get them, anyway. You know that. Sooner or later."

No sound. No movement. No change in the tone of his voice. But now the prisoner was dead. *Your people got him*; that had been her Nunc Dimittus. Valdes, also, was nodding gravely. She had done well; very well indeed.

"Fuck the bitch," the Colonel said, straightening up.

The sergeant followed him out into the passage. Bellido was the first—as was proper—to get out the tobacco; they rolled their cigarettes and lit them from the sergeant's cheap metal lighter, both standing with their backs against the wall, legs astraddle. Now, briefly, rank could be forgotten. Ramona was dead, and they were the only two mourners. They would smoke their cigarettes there, in the passage, slowly—as was decent—and then they would go.

"It's funny," Valdes said, "how they always want to *know*."

"Yes. Curiosity is one of the last things to go. That, when you think about it, augurs rather well for the human race."

"She might have hung on, if you hadn't told her."

The Colonel shrugged. "When it's over, it's over."

"Yes," the sergeant said.

Then, after a minute or so,

"It's bad, though. Not having a priest."

"There's always a priest, if they want one. She didn't."

"It's bad, though."

"Yes," the Colonel said. "It's bad."

He looked down at the inch of cigarette-stub glowing between his fingers. There had to be more to life than that. People weren't cigarette-ends. That was obvious. And yet the fact remained that she'd done well; very well indeed. It didn't make sense. It was over. That was all you could say. And you didn't go on when it was over. Clearly there were things she had known ... where the others were hiding, perhaps, which way they were planning to escape ... but that was just information. Knowing that would save no one's life. You didn't use the brushes and the hooks to find out *that* sort of thing. But if life is no more than a glow between one's fingers, what distinguishes the one from the other? To the prisoner, all had been the same. That was really the trouble. Bellido didn't understand.

"And the others?"

"What about them?"

"D'you reckon we'll catch them?"

"Yes," Bellido said. *"Claro que sí."*

The truth of the matter was, he wasn't sure. The cordon techniques had been developed over the years; in Spain they were ninety-five per cent efficient. But this wasn't really Spain. This was the Costa del Sol. They weren't marking the road from Bujalance to Montoro, where a plume of dust signals the arrival of an ox-cart; they were marking the four-lane Malaga highway, where a thousand cars pass every forty minutes. Cars registered, moreover, in every province in Spain and in every damned country in Western Europe. If the cordons didn't work, then in the morning the dragnet would go down. The investigation would begin. It might turn up something, but it wouldn't turn up those others. The police were efficient, but slow; the others were efficient and fast. There was no denying it.

"There'll be nothing doing till the morning, anyway," he said. "We may as well get some sleep."

Except that he wouldn't sleep. He couldn't. If he did, the nightmares would come. Back in Madrid, with his wife and four children, he knew he'd be all right again; but right now, he couldn't sleep alone.

He dropped his cigarette to the floor and set his foot on it. He didn't think the others would be getting much sleep tonight, either. But there was little consolation to be found in that.

Only when he bit into the apple was Henry aware of his

178

own hunger. It didn't occur to him, though, when he had finished the apple to search for more food; he left the core lying on the white vinyl top of the kitchenette table, took the glass of milk and carried it carefully across the sitting-room and through the splintered wooden door of the bedroom. Anita was sitting on the bed, fixing her dress with safety-pins she had found. "It's so hot," she said. "Can't I open the windows?" She took the glass and started to drink. "I'll have to turn the lights off," Henry said. She nodded. He went back to thumb down the light switch; then walked past the bed, hands outstretched in the darkness, to pull back the curtains and open the sliding windows. It was certainly very hot in the penthouse; something had perhaps gone wrong with the air conditioning system; opening the window, he felt at once the relative coolness of the night air on his sweat-dampened forehead and cheeks. Light was still spilling from the buildings and the street beneath him and black, foreshortened figures still moved to and fro; but elsewhere it was very dark, the hills to the north lost against the hugeness of the sky. A thin cloud, a gathering of stars. Slowly, though, his eyes grew accustomed to the darkness, so that looking back he could make out the paleness of the bedroom walls, the whiteness of the turned-back sheets and looming over them, at the head of the bed, the darker, motionless shape that had to be Anita. The shape seemed, at least, to be motionless; but then he heard the dry clink as she put down the empty glass on the night table. Light was filtering into the room through the cracked door; otherwise, surely, there'd be total darkness. "It's dark tonight," he said; and then, "Do you want to go to sleep?" She didn't answer. He looked out of the window again, watching a car quest slowly up the road, its indicator flashing, then walked back round the bed; his eye caught, as he went, an indeterminate blur of movement and the glass broke sharply on the floor. She said something under her breath, probably a swearword.

179

"Did you want anything else?" He had stopped, his hands hanging loosely at his thighs. "Sorry," Anita said. "I was getting my feet up." He walked on and sat down on the edge of the bed beside her. "I didn't think it'd be this dark. I can hardly see you. Just the dress ... Velvet, isn't it? Black, anyway." His fingers lifted the hem where it fell just clear of her knee, assessing the thickness, the texture of the material. "I'm sorry it ... I suppose you can have it mended?" Still she didn't reply. He could hear the sound of her breathing; light, fast, shallow. He didn't like the sound of her breathing. He wanted the sound of her voice. In this darkness, a contact had been lost; he wanted her back again. But he didn't want to speak again himself, either. He didn't know why not. He was tired, perhaps. Tired of talking, anyway. In the darkness, his eyelids felt heavy. His hand rested, relaxed, on the unexpectedly sharp curve of her knee. He wondered what the time was. He felt tired and heavy. He wanted sleep. But that would be dangerous. She might get up and go. He couldn't trust her. There was no one he could trust. He could rest, though. He wouldn't sleep. He took away his hand. She didn't move then; but he saw, when he stretched himself out beside her, the pale blur of her face turn towards him. Could you say you could see a face when you only saw a face? No expression, no movement of eyes and mouth, but just an oval blur? No. He couldn't see her. But contact had been re-established. It was there with the warmth of her body under his hand, with the soft smoothness of velvet. Holding her like this, she couldn't escape. "No," she said, very softly. "Oh no. Please, no." He couldn't think what she meant.

Then later,
"I think there are skins," Henry said. "The mind has skins, like an onion. There's an inner mind and an outer

mind. And then your clothes ... Clothes are to hide you. Know what I mean?"

"Isn't that what Freud said?"

"I don't mean it like that."

On his feet, without his clothes, he stared into the mirror. But the room was dark still and the mirror showed him only the featureless blur of his body; his face was shadowed, invisible. The carpet felt soft, though, under his bare feet; the carpet was real. From behind him there came from time to time a small, abrupt glow; Anita, lying on the bed and smoking a cigarette.

"Uniforms. They show the way you *want* to be. I always wanted to wear a uniform."

"That's silly."

"But then you take off your clothes and you're all the same. And that's the whole idea of a uniform, isn't it? I'd never thought of it that way before."

"Men and women aren't the same."

"Yes, they are. In the way I mean. That's why it's never any good."

He went back to the bed and sat down again beside her, close beside her; his hand resting with confidence this time, as it were naturally, on the soft flattened curve of her belly; a different softness there, a different warmth, and yet he knew he was right. It was all the same. And that explained it. "You don't ask anything. I like that."

"What ought I to ask?"

"It's just that I can't. I never could. That's all there is to it."

"Don't *you* ask yourself ... anything?"

"Yes. But not now. Not this time. I don't have to, with you. I know now why it is. That's what's so good about it."

"Henry, I wish you'd told me. I wish I could have helped you."

"You have. You *are* helping me. I think I love you. If

181

I love anybody. There again . . . I never have."

"But if . . . Oh, God. All those *people* down there. It's just too late. And you, you're so *gentle*. It doesn't make sense."

He rolled over, as before, to lie beside her, his head on the pillow touching her hair. She was right. It didn't make sense. That was the important thing. At last, she'd understood.

"They had a drawn sword between them. In bed."

"Who did?"

"Tristan, wasn't it? And Isolde. It's an opera."

"What's that got to do with anything?"

"They had it between them, you see. Sort of symbolic."

"But it's not like that at all."

"I suppose not."

Too late. She was right about that, too. It was too late, even if they ran.

"You kissed me then, didn't you? And I felt all those things I think I'm supposed to feel. It was fine. Where do you get this drawn-sword stuff?"

"I don't feel anything much," Henry said.

"But you're tired, you've been . . . Well, what *do* you feel?"

"It's like I said. This is the mountain top. If I can't do it now. I never will. And if we go down, they'll catch us." Henry lifted one arm, looked at the luminous dial of his wrist-watch. "We're going to have to kill ourselves," he said.

Silence and darkness. Only the luminous dial, spinning like a wheel.

"I can't, Henry. I'm a coward. I don't *want* to."

"It's not a matter of wanting to."

"But you could escape. If you did, I'd join you later. Anywhere. You have to *try*, Henry. You can't kill yourself like Hitler in a . . . bloody bunker."

"It's not just me any more. It's both of us. Can't you *see*?"

It was odd. He was sure that she'd understood. But the panic was back in her voice now; she was frightened again. "You don't really mean it. You said you ... Henry, you *can't.*"

"We won't talk about it," Henry said gently.

Yes, better not talk about it. Then he'd forget it. He didn't really mean it; these were just ideas that came and went, peeled off like the onion-skin. He wasn't sane. The awful thing was that she, on the other hand, had finally seen the truth; she was tired of sanity. If he escaped, she'd join him; anywhere. When you see the truth, you can speak it. Not before. And then it's too late. Anita turned her face sideways on the pillow and felt a tear roll gently, caressingly, down her cheek. Beyond the open window and reflected in her tears were the first vague suspicions of the coming daylight.

Henry sat at the end of the bed, his shoulders hunched, the Luger in his hands. He rocked himself gently to and fro. Anita's dress lay on the floor at his feet, crumpled up in the slow grey vibrations of the dawn; Anita herself lay on the bed, the sheet drawn not quite up to her shoulders. She, too, seemed to be crumpled, to be smaller than usual, a child in a cot; she was asleep. He watched her.

The Luger in his hands felt heavy and cold.

He wondered whether or not to do it now, while she was asleep. That would be the gentlest way. And he was, after all, a gentle person.

But then he saw that she wasn't, in fact, asleep; her dark eyes were regarding him from under their swollen lids, her head had moved a little on the pillow. At the corner of her wide mouth he could see a smear of milk. He turned towards her, leaning over her, and she herself

183

pulled down the sheet, rolling over as she did so on to her back, raising and opening her knees; her lifted arms were round and white in the shadows. Embracing him, her hands travelled slowly over his back and he felt himself rising to her, himself becoming tall and hard, a tree reaching for the sky, for the grey light. Her different softness. Her warmth. Her mouth. The dry metallic *click* of her kiss.

He stared down at the Luger in his hands. His thumb rested on the safety catch. He had just flicked it off.

You see I knew a long while back my father never really liked me. There was something he wanted to tell me or show me or somebody so I thought he did. That was when I was small. Ever since then I didn't expect anyone to like me.

I thought I was maybe a bit odd, nobody liking me. What I see now very clearly and what I wanted to write down was, I was wrong about that. People don't like other people, not really. I see now that's what this sex thing is all about, I was mistaken about that too.

I mean if you go to bed with someone and you say "I love you" and so on, you forget about not liking people. That's what I didn't see before. You say "I love you" to yourself, really, or anyway it's yourself you're fooling. That's what was wrong with me. I couldn't fool myself but I couldn't quite see the truth about it, either. Once you realise people don't like other people, everything falls into place. All the cruelty, and the starving people in India and everything.

I always wanted to like people. I don't know why, it seems silly now. And the way they talked to me in London, it all had to do with liking people and seeing that they got their rights. Looking back they didn't seem to like me but then as I said I didn't expect anyone to. It was the same here though with Cipriano and Ramona.

184

You're the only one who's ever liked me. I knew that when I wouldn't let them kill you. I didn't know before. That seems funny, too.

He had taken from the bedroom wardrobe Santi's dressing-gown, a splendid silken thing of many-coloured stripes. The sleeves rustled irritably, however, against the surface of the table as he wrote, distracting his thoughts. He frowned at the paper in front of him, smooth and white, ruled with blue feint lines that seemed, as he stared at them, to undulate like the waves on the seashore, to move in slow relays towards him with the ceaseless, aimless rhythm of breaking combers. The words, too, blue-black scribblings on the page, caught in that ebb and flow, drifting to the pull of invisible planets. But there was a meaning there, a meaning at last, a meaning to that pulsing of slow dark tides. Leaning forwards, his frown deepening, he began with great care to write again.

You know when you want to protect people. I want to do that, but it's awful knowing that people don't like you and even want to kill you. There isn't anything else much to like except the sex business and that doesn't work for us, not now that we know, and if you went to bed with anyone else I couldn't stand it, not your going to bed with someone who didn't like you. Santiago didn't like you. I'm glad he's dead, in fact I'm glad about it all in a way. It had to happen so I could know what I know now. Cipriano said even if you run, well, I think he knew, too.

He underlined the words *even if you run*, because they seemed to him important. Twenty minutes later, he added the words,

That's all.

—and put down the pen.

"We ought to get dressed," Henry said.

He felt more cheerful now. It had helped, getting it all

down on paper. An effort, yes, but well worth it. It gave you a certain sense of satisfaction, knowing that everything at last had been explained. It was important, after all, that people should understand, and it was all so simple once you understood it. His eyes pained him a little, but that didn't matter. Not now.

"It's no good," Anita said. "I can't do it."

"I'll do it. First you, then me."

"Do it now, then, *now*, get *on* with it."

She didn't scream this time, or even raise her voice; her tone was almost conversational. Her face had no colour, only contour. The cheekbones stood out. The big eyes were sunken. The sun would bring back colour to her face, but the sun hadn't yet risen.

"We have to get dressed first."

"Why?"

He hadn't really thought about it.

"It's more dignified," he said.

The pistol was in his hands, but didn't feel heavy any more; throughout the long night it had become a part of him, an extension not so much of his body as of his will, the means to an inevitable end. This end Anita seemed to have recognised. She didn't stare at the pistol any more. It was there simply as he was there, inseparable from him, as godhead resides in the host. It was useless to stare at it. You could only see *it*, not what it meant. "I don't want to die," Anita said. "Not even if you do it."

"But what else *is* there? After this?"

He was genuinely puzzled. He had been so sure that she had understood. He put the pistol down on the night table. Lying there, it was still part of him, of *them*, of their promised death; he took off the dressing-robe and stood by the table, by the pistol, by the telephone, tall, naked, looking sternly down at her, folding the dressing-robe over his left arm. It was over. She had to see that. There was nothing else. Death was neatness, was orderliness; it tidied things up. That was what *dignified* meant. Everything proper and correct, everything in its place. Santiago, on the floor; his dressing-robe—loose ends of sash tucked into its pockets—back on its hanger in the wardrobe. He turned to swing open the wardrobe door and re-hung the robe, carefully. Attention to detail. That was what you looked for. Behind the robe he saw a sharp circle of white outlined in the dimness, disturbing him, reminding him of something, of what...? He reached out and took it from the peg. A white Nazi officer's cap.

Strange.

"This is mine," he said.

He stepped back and turned, peering at the shiny skull-and-crossbones above the peak. A small hole with charred edges, like a cigarette-burn, appeared in the flat white disc directly above it; he stared at it, still mystified, while out of the open wardrobe a booming cataract of sound and of inexplicable pain cascaded over him, drenching him with sweat on the instant. The door, swinging back, struck him hard, the moving mirror giving him a fogged glimpse of Anita lying on the bed with the Luger in her hand; then the wall of iron-hard vibrations ran into him again and the mirror shattered to pieces. With the cap in his hand, he started to walk towards the door, slowly, with measured paces; his eyes were bulging in the expectation of a third shattering impact, but it didn't come. "Mine," he said. The surprise had gone from his voice; it was an affirmation. He walked through the splintered door.

Santiago and his friend Cipriano lay on the floor, waiting for him patiently. Beyond the penthouse windows were the Andalusian hills, touched on their western slopes with the first brightness and the first shadows of the coming day, and the white houses and slanted villas of Torrevedra; before long the sprinklers would be turning, the early cars heading down the road to the beaches. A thread of blood ran out of Henry's mouth. He put the cap on his head and went to the other door.

Beyond it, the long, empty passage.

He walked on, and for a long time; a naked, gangling figure with the cap perched at a jaunty angle on his head and with blood trickling from his mouth in a steady, pulsing stream. His bare feet left sticky, blackish-red prints on the floor, irregularly spaced. Whether he looked dignified or ridiculous, only an outside observer could have said; and in the passage was no such observer. Henry was alone, and slowly dying. He was the whole of mankind; as such, he had no conscious thoughts. He could hear, as his knees began to tremble, the noise of a motorcar engine building up to a whining crescendo, the grind of brakes, the ting of a telephone bell, but these were noises only, devoid of any accompanying images, as were the other, profounder noises inside him; two bullets had torn holes in his quivering lungs and there the air wheezed, the blood bubbled. Still he kept on walking. He had no choice.

An empty bottle of milk stood on the kitchen table; an empty bottle, and an apple core that was rapidly turning brown.

Anita lay on the bed, on her side, knees drawn up, head lowered; she held the pistol tightly, cuddled it like a baby, its muzzle pressing against her left breast. Around the angled trigger her finger was curved. And *now*, she said to herself, *now*; knowing very well that she wouldn't. Fragments of the broken mirror shone in the gathering sunlight.

AUTHOR'S NOTE

Some attention to detail is always desirable even in a work of fantasy, and in the original typescript of *Take My Drum to England* the method of making gelignite and the technique employed by Henry and Cipriano in detonating it by telephone were both precisely described. I am very grateful, in this connection, for the help of Mr. Arthur Peterson and Sr. Delgado (of the Spanish telephone service) with whom these matters were discussed exhaustively. But having satisfied myself that the whole thing is feasible, I now feel that to include this kind of information in a work of fiction—or indeed in any book at all—would be ill-advised. Many people seem only too anxious to turn the most preposterous of fantasies into fact, as the last ten years have witnessed, and Henry Allanbee is not supposed to be an altogether impossible figure. I must make it clear to anyone who may be tempted to put any such a technique into practice that only an experienced communications engineer (such as Cipriano) would be likely to meet with any sort of success and, moreover, that such indications as I have given here are in several instances deliberately misleading. It may well seem to the ordinary reader that such precautions are in themselves a little absurd, but I wouldn't want even a quite extraordinary one to blow himself unnecessarily into smithereens. I don't have all that many readers I can spare. *Take My Drum to England* is based on an original scheme, and in particular on a central character, created by Mr. Peter Duffell. For the idea and for his further comments I am also most grateful.

D.C.

TAKE MY DRUM
TO ENGLAND

Desmond Cory—an explorer of weird worlds. In *Deadfall*, that of the professional jewel thief; in *The Night Hawk*, that of the political assassin. *Take My Drum to England* masterfully maps his weirdest and most terrible world to date—that of the bomber, the hijacker, the social reject who builds an illusion of power out of a suitcase filled with gelignite. Not since *Brighton Rock* has the topsy-turvy rationality of the psychotic been so convincingly depicted.

Henry Allanbee, a young man in search of a Cause, finds his in the great thirty-year-old one of the Spanish Republic. His obscure urge to destroy is channelled into the near-respectable course of a political assignment. In addition to his box of detonators, Henry now carries a license to assassinate—and the plans are laid by cool-headed professionals.

Only when the plans go wrong does Henry's puritanical self-righteousness turn into something far more frightening; as the police move in he finds himself trapped hopelessly in a psychological labyrinth. Sex and violence—with Cory as with few other writers—are the true mainspring of suspense rather than an additional seasoning, and with *Take My Drum to England* the springs are wound up to snapping point. Yet again ... a thriller for the connoisseur.